POPULAR FORMS FOR A RADICAL THEATRE

Edited by Caridad Svich and Sarah Ruhl

NoPassport Press
Theatre & Performance Texts

NoPassport Press
Theatre & Performance Texts
Edition 2011 by NoPassport Press
PO Box 1786, South Gate, CA 90280 USA;
NoPassportPress@aol.com
Website: www.nopassport.org
ISBN: 978-0-578-09809-8

NoPassport

No Passport is a Pan-American theatre alliance & press devoted to live, virtual and print action, advocacy, and change toward the fostering of cross-cultural diversity in the arts with an emphasis on the embrace of the hemispheric spirit in US Latina/o and Latin-American theatre-making.

NoPassport Press' Theatre & Performance PlayTexts Series and its Dreaming the Americas Series promotes new writing for the stage, texts on theory and practice, and theatrical translations. NoPassport is a sponsored project of Fractured Atlas. All tax-exempt donations may be made to http://www.fracturedatlas.org/donate/2623

This volume, in part, was previously published as special issue of *Contemporary Theatre Review Volume 16, No. 3* (August 2006), Taylor & Francis Publishers/UK, and is reprinted with the journal's permission and with the authors' permission.

Contents

Popular Forms for a Radical Theatre

Caridad Svich

The investigation and critique of popular cultural forms has been a significant constant of contemporary art practice for the last fifty years. Visual artists, novelists, interdisciplinary performers and composers have been at the forefront of such investigation. Within the last fifteen years in the English-speaking theatre especially there has been increasing discussion and experimentation with forms dis-used, old, and ancient as a way of interfacing with new technologies and the expectations of late 20th-early 21st century audiences. Practitioners have been expressing a desire to re-connect with the audience in a populist manner as an unveiled rejection of the avant-garde's perceived 'contempt' of the audience. Working both within and against the commercial grain, and the pervasive affect of junk culture, theatre artists are pulling apart and/or resurrecting old forms of popular entertainment to tell stories anew in a provocative manner, and thus reawaken the radical impulse in performance.

The meaning of radicalism in theatre and performance shifts with every generation. However, at its root are sceptic empiricism, a spirit of reform and/or revolution, and a departure from orthodoxy in practice, concept or design. Resisting definition, 'the radical' lives in both the 'high' and 'low' system of differentiation established by a culture. Moreover, the binary fix that once determined high and low forms has shifted from one century to the other and indeed post post-modernism, the 'popular' has been reconsidered (in terms of its relational aspects) in regard to or exclusion from the canon, whether the practitioners are already populist artists, provocative or belong to the patrician elite. Work that ruptures existing traditions, upends convention, brings together disparate energies into cohesion, or markedly shifts the perspective and point of view of an audience and/or witness to a performance event is radical without the necessity of containing material that goes against-the-grain of popular sentiment. Bakhtin's concept of the carnivalesque included, after all, the language of the marketplace which disrupted the privileged order of polite speech, rituals and games that often centred on the genital zones, and popular festive forms where modes of behaviour and ideals were inverted or subverted. By rethinking the popular, then, today's practitioners are enacting a hegemonic and counter-hegemonic struggle that engages a Gramscian 'repertoire of resistance' that is marked by constant negotiation.

In this volume, established and emerging (mostly) Anglo-American practitioners wrestle with the contradictory impulses of creating work that resists orthodoxy and its domain of signs but also embraces its formal and emotive power. In fact, there is a lively recognition amongst the artists gathered here that what have become conventional or standardised signs of culture and performance should be 'used' (in a market value manner) precisely to liberate, disrupt and re-order the reading and receiving of work, especially in a globalised culture that is signified by the deterritorialization, and the real and imagined repatriation of citizens of the geopolitical community. Indeed, it should be noted that there are great, many artists working in non-English-language theatre who are making texts and pieces that are responding to this populist/provocative paradigm in striking, unusual and admittedly more radical ways. However, a choice has been made with this volume to centre on transatlantic practitioners as a way to witness regional (in the global landscape) commonalities and shared differences within those working in particularly dominant media-driven cultures.

In the wake of 9/11, the war in Iraq, and the natural tragedies in Asia and the US, the rise of a new political theatre has surfaced.

While in the UK, there is a strong and reinvigorated tradition of topical theatre, which on occasion can also be political theatre, artists in the US have been grappling with on the one hand, the responsibility and demands of fact-based and mainly journalistic-in-approach theatre of testimony (i.e. *The Exonerated,* 2002), and on the other, freer, more provocative and frank responses to the current sociopolitical climate (i.e. Jose Rivera's *Massacre,* 2005, Stephen Adley Guirgis' *The Last Days of Judas Iscariot,* 2005). Neither extreme is the answer. Topical work, however, that is comfortable exuding and proclaiming its own topicality is basically just another form of reportage, and not an act of cultural examination, which is what ultimately and at its moral best (and I mean 'moral' in the absolute sense as opposed to how some of our political leaders and culture-makers have used the word) theatre requires. If theatre is to rise, as it must, to speak to a culture then it must do so from a position not of indifference and decadence, but rather from a moral one – urging and emphasising participation, and broadening communication. In fact, many artists are looking outside the prescribed, journalistically driven forms to shape a theatre that is grass roots in appeal and makeup. There has been a steady return to street performances, guerrilla theatre, and anti-theatrical events situated in non-traditional spaces. Practitioners are taking to the 'streets' for inspiration and the effect can be witnessed in works that borrow heavily and freely from cultures outside the canonically text-based tradition.

While the mini-rage of New Vaudevillians (i.e. clowns Bill Irwin, Geoff Hoyle, David Shiner) has long since passed, the spirit of vaudeville and cabaret is significantly evident in the performance styles of established companies The Wooster Group, Anne Bogart's SITI, UK's Improbable Theatre, and Forced Entertainment. On their heels are young equally disparate companies like Austin-based Rude Mechanicals, New York City's Elevator Repair Service, Radiohole and The Civilians, and UK's Shunt, as well as solo performers like US' Reverend Billy, and UK's Ricardo Dedomenici, who work with the raw energies, presentational style, 'accidental' methodologies, and populist ambitions of early vaudeville and political cabaret to re-fuel the dramatic form with varying degrees of artistic success. Historian and playwright Charles L. Mee, Jr. is also a major influence on a new generation of theatre artists, who are inspired by his collage techniques, and appropriation and re-sampling of Pop culture icons and motifs through his re-workings of classic texts. The phenomenon of hip-hop (both in its commercialised and non-commercialised forms) continues to mark US theatre in divergent, problematic and envigorating ways. Interactive club forms like karaoke (i.e. Diane Paulus' *The Karaoke Show*) and new burlesque, as well as the use of techniques and genres from popular film are increasingly part of the vocabulary of the current generation of theatre-makers who are rooted deeply in the contemporary condition, and are trying to reconnect to a society that seems distant and alienated from its theatre-makers and the works being made.

Form for form's sake alone is not what is at stake in this new generation of writing and performance, but rather the search for and making of community. Although it is disingenuous to think that community can happen in a night, and certainly the word 'community' is so over-used now that it risks losing its true meaning altogether, practitioners who are awake and awakened by their cultural moment and responding to the visions and messages that need be sent back to culture (in shamanistic terms) are staking a claim toward the progressive power of performance and story-telling. They are asking the questions that need be asked especially at a time when cultures are forcibly splintered by war, violence, the uses and abuses of the corporate machine, and the casual and infecting inertia of lax cultural power brokers driven by a bottom line that has everything to do with keeping brands alive and not art. How then does an artist now effectively communicate with an audience? What tools can be brought to bear to tell radical stories in a manner that is connected and in concert with culture? And in the tail end of the age of replication and reproduction, what images can be newly minted against the received signs engrained in culture?

In this issue, the theatre profession takes charge, as practitioners, theatre makers, programmers and professional critics speak to these questions in their own unique ways. Iconoclastic dramatist W. David Hancock opens the issue with a challenge to theatres to fulfill their promise of Democracy and offer art that is for everyone. He extols the virtue of the Horatios of this theatre world, who can and do make new visions for a tired, chaotic time – who can see past the wreckage left by Hamlet (in his example) and report on it with truth, imagination and the freedom of the uncensored poetic voice. Co-editor Sarah Ruhl diagrams the effects of a mash-up culture driven to seemingly endless acts of reruns and recycling. She offers that the ardor of the poetic voice conveyed through a specific form in its very sacredness (un-mashed-up, pure and true to itself) can be of lasting value to a culture and theatrical art form itself, and its future. Todd London, artistic director of New York City's New Dramatists, picks up both Hancock's and Ruhl's lead to embrace the specificity of place in American theatre as a way of looking beyond and off the map of 'official' theatrical production. London understands that theatre is by its nature local, and that only in 20th-century American theatre (and I would extend that to UK theatre as well which has been hobbled by the celebrity factor in recent years) has there been an irregular and unfortunate shift toward a theatre dominated by greed for more and more audiences.

Balancing London's forthright essay is Dijana Milosevic's interview with Eugenio Barba on the 40th anniversary of Odin Teatret, and composer Michael Friedman's playful examination of cabaret. In Barba's case, the responsibility of the artist lies in paying attention to both the little histories (personal and specific) within the context of the big Histories. He evaluates the impact of a third theatre next to that of a theatre made to the specifications and expectations of society. Friedman focuses on cabaret as impulse for a form of drama that acts as a 'third' gender, as it were, to narrative-bound entertainments, and acts of literary provocation. For Friedman, the little histories (to use Barba's term) enacted by cabaret artists are evidence of positive resistance against hegemony and the non-market value of failure. It is precisely the tension between success and failure, professionalism and amateurism, high-tech and lo-fi aesthetics that demarcate the liminal space where much of the new theatre, the Horatio-inspired, anti-mass market, community-centred work lives at its best and fullest.

Looking at mainstream theatre, critic Aleks Sierz observes how the possibilities for radicalism through popular theatrical forms can be reinvigorated in new British theatre writing. Taking a broad and lucid survey of works from the Traverse Theatre in Scotland, the Royal Court, the Royal National Theatre of London, Soho Theatre, and the Bush, he cites reasons for optimism in the notion of theatre artists deconstructing left-wing populist work of the past to stimulate, especially in the wake of 9/11 and the Iraq war, a staying trend for relevant political theatre in the UK. Relevancy is currency in the work of Frantic Assembly, whose co-founder Scott Graham is interviewed here by Soho Theatre's Nina Steiger. In anticipation of the premiere of *On Blindness*, a three-way co-production between Frantic Asembly, Paines Plough and Graeae hosted by the Soho Theatre Company, Graham speaks to the pleasures and pitfalls of collaboration and devising in the development of new plays, and

Frantic Assembly's ongoing commitment to pop culture. A company devoted to its young core audience and collaborating inventively with playwrights and musicians, Frantic Assembly's understanding that 'theatre exists between performers, lighting, the audience and music' is key to the wide-ranging conversation of how often the benchmarks of the process are outside the practice hall – in culture, alive and kicking.

Past and present collide in a short piece by American critic Jonathan Kalb, who offers a meditation on multi-media's power in theatre as a vital agent for intimacy and truth. Opera and theatre director Diane Paulus follows Kalb's provocations with a passionate-clear-eyed take on the role of the audience in a theatre designed along both populist and provocative lines. She discusses the making and staging of two of her most successful theatrical cultural experiments *The Donkey Show* and *The Karaoke Show,* both of which are loose adaptations of Shakespeare's *A Midsummer Night's Dream* and *The Comedy of Errors,* respectively. Through the explication of her work, Paulus magnifies the audience's position in creating the theatrical experience, and indeed altering pre-rehearsed performances by their interaction. Paulus seeks to investigate the process of interactivity as a means of recontextualising process and practice.

A conversation/performance piece by Richard Maxwell and actor Brian Mendes as they talk karaoke in a Brooklyn café continues Paulus' position on populism and performance. Through their halting, chatty, alternately bemused and focused conversation Maxwell and Mendes speak about acting, and debate the consequences of ironic representation on stage. Richard Maxwell is a practitioner who seems to embody the many conflicting impulses alive in today's theatre and performance. His emotive texts are performed un-emotively in what has become a signature style for Maxwell: flat, American, uninflected, and static. His work is broken by bursts of music, movement and dance, and his impact on a new wave of dramatic writing is strikingly evident. You need only witness the works of post-grunge dramatist Adam Rapp, neo-realist writers Jessica Goldberg and Annie Baker and droll formalist Will Eno to see the imprint of Maxwell (who is imprinted perhaps unconsciously by the film work of auteur Hal Hartley) on a new generation of theatre artists. The irreverent conversation between Maxwell and Mendes, long time collaborators, offers a vivid glimpse into the process of practitioners living in the heat of their cultural moment outside of 'knee-jerk' reactions to events in society. It also sheds light on their respect for the power of making a mistake in front of an audience who already knows the musical score (as in karaoke) and what that means, in a greater sense, toward the actual shaping of a theatre performance. Mendes and Maxwell debate the value and de-valued nature of the presentational style favored by nouveau cabaret-vaudeville-inspired theatre-makers and performers (and which karaoke players reinforce). Should greatness be a key toward judging a performance? And what measure of greatness is linked to falseness? The burden of success and its trappings of comfort come up again, as it does in so many of the pieces herein, against the standards of failure, and working on the brink.

Shifting through the cultural exhaust of their times, practitioners who are invested in the active present of their society and its future are divesting themselves of the marginalist badge that has been conveniently placed on them by society's operators and are slowly taking command of their cultural moment. Whether it be through the rigorous excavation and exploration of old performance forms in order to comprehend their meaning to society and/or their true origin, or through provocative works fueled by intellectual curiosity and governed by metaphor, artists are refusing to perpetuate the making of cultural junk, which is often dressed and disguised in impressive and intimidating finery, and instead be popular culture's expressive artery system, and very life-blood.

After all, popular culture is not just Pop. It is our languages, politics, fashion, television, sports, music, film, religion – in effect, the very elements that hold a culture in common together. And this commonality includes points of divergence, difference, and even outmodedness. Practitioners and scholars have the responsibility therefore to speak to their culture directly. That is their job. Our job. To keep our ear to the ground, to listen attentively, to witness, and to observe the patterns and variations. From our acts of listening and witnessing and observance then we must record, document, and then transform acts of culture, random or otherwise, into art which through both form and content, because one does not exist independently of the other (as so many cultural pundits profess), investigates who we are and how we are and challenges society to move forward, to truly progress, rather than regress into repetitive acts of cultural amnesia.

In the end, what threads the quest for re-connection and relevancy in this volume is how to make 'real' work and what does it mean to live in real time, and be of your time. Whether using interactive software, multi-media, age-old striptease, panto, or left-wing issue-driven theatre, the primacy of the moment is what is important. An artist has to be able to catch the moment, as it were, to capture it, on the wing. Quality of time and perception, acute listening, and a willingness to regard and take in the 'other' are chief attributes of art-making that enable (rather than disable, which is what much of the detritus in our culture encourages) a culture, a society, to see itself anew, unfamiliar, and strange. "How strange we are," an audience must say after a performance. "How wonderfully, woefully strange. How much more must we do to truly move forward." Experimental playwright Will Eno, in his essay-letter on form, playfully and movingly champions the multiplicity of human existence as the fundamental barometer for art and its making. He reminds us that content and form are of a piece, and need be understood as such for a work of art to communicate. Out of the randomness that seems to assemble us in this world, art has the courage to at the very least make a mere semblance of order. Art offers shape and form, and through it we take the pulse of our moral compass.

A democratic theatre

W. David Hancock

Prior to 1900, physicists believed that we could measure space and time independently. Einstein taught us that space and time are inseparable. Oddly, most theatre artists still operate using pre-20th century physics: they create live events in which space and time are distinct, measurable quantities. In fact, many basic artistic concepts long ago embraced by your average high school teacher are, for some reason, ignored by many of the American theatre's most entrenched and influential practitioners, educators and institutions. Theatre is maturing into a dead art form because, by and large, our established practitioners have neither the will nor the imaginations to create new dramatic forms that accurately reflect the newest intellectual frontiers of humanity. By choosing to cling to antiquated belief systems, playwrights are losing their historical authority to anticipate the future. Our theatres, our processes of making and developing new work, our systems of funding are so grounded in long disproven fallacies that we have started to forget the very scent of drama.

Regional American theatres, originally founded on the ideals of Democracy and the promise of art for everyone, have evolved into houses of elitism and exclusivity. American Realism, the virus hatched in these incubators, continues to infect our collective imagination and inhibit our cultural progress. The spiritual danger to Realism is that the form can only function through the withholding of information. Dramatic action, those petty on-stage conflicts that the Realists would like us to believe are the heart and soul of a play, are only made possible through a complicit distortion of point-of-view and by limiting and controlling the audience's access to its own humanity. In realistic plays, basic human truths are heavily guarded by a self-anointed master class of playwrights, designers and directors. This invisible cabal does its best to define the human experience for us and they dole out their holy secrets from the altar, using inbred theatrical techniques similar to those of religious oligarchies. Not only is the world of these plays pawned off as an accurate representation of a universal reality, but, as with many sermons, the events of the play are placed in a bogus but emotionally provocative causal relationship. Realistic scenes pretend to be happening in front of us for the first and only time and, faced with this urgency, we become hopelessly tangled in the maze of the on stage story — rather than being reminded of our own complicity in the real world events that the drama is representing. In a realistic drama, we only get to see what the playwright and director want us to see. All scenes that contradict the artistic agenda of the makers are jettisoned in the production process. The audience is forced to experience the psychological revelations that best prove the pseudoscience of those in charge.

When playwrights do begin to ask legitimate and important questions about the human condition, a distinctly American play development model forces them into a world of "pay-offs" and "character investment", corporate techniques that force an audience to look for answers in the play instead of inside themselves. Young theatre artists, born with the passion and drive to move our culture forward are coerced into believing that their natural brilliance and unique vision is actually a problem that must be fixed. Droves of potential Beckets and Strindbergs either leave the field altogether or end up as bitter and disgruntled ex-makers, stuck in artistically compromised jobs at the very institutions they once lived in opposition to. Even the occasional quasi-experimental play traveling the regional theatre circuit functions like Carnival in a dictatorship. We have our one day a year to get drunk and make public fun of the government, before we return to the dreary and highly controlled status quo.

Thankfully, the occasional radical will emerge in this darkness, a populist able to use the tools of the oligarchy to tell the truth instead of obfuscating it. Perhaps these uncommon theatre artists are best represented by the character of Horatio in *Hamlet*. He's not the hero, but he is the one who survives the chaos and helps us understand why the hero fell. As an extension of the playwright, Horatio is the portal into the world of the play and — reliable or unreliable — he's the only witness who feels compelled to tell us what happened. True, Horatio's tale is only a version of the truth, but his is a story that is aware of its own fallibility. By endowing the play with a self-conscious point-of-view, Horatio constantly reminds the audience that what they are witnessing is a recreation of an event which has already happened — one which will happen again if we are not eternally vigilant. Simply put, Horatio allows us to grapple with stories that are greater than our own life experience and thus beyond our ability to control. By looking deep into the Horatio-portal the theatre artist becomes a maker of their time and place, not just a consequence of their time and place. We recover the possibility of making a true Democratic theatre, where characters have free-will and where epiphany replaces forced accumulation.

Alarmingly, even Horatio is losing his ability to bring us out of our cultural slumber. Culturally significant points of view, once the domain of artists, theologians and intellectuals, are now owned by software companies, television networks and commercial film studios. We can no longer use the magic mirror to peer in on Hamlet because the technology is no longer in the public domain, all such relics having been bought by Disney years ago. Part of this disturbing trend is Horatio's own fault, of course: he's become far too self-involved to serve as Hamlet's straight man. "I've felt disenfranchised for years," he tells the audience, "and I want to tell my own life story tonight." Indeed, the more insignificant live theatre becomes to our culture — the more each playwright calls out with, "pay attention to me!" — the less likely Horatio will be willing to serve up Hamlet's tragedy. To open the portal, Horatio must be humble; he must focus the attention to others. He is the cheerleader, not the quarterback, and he must be willing to leave the field a bloody mess at the end of the game.

The essays in this book are by and about a group of radical populists who are struggling to regain ownership of what should be a free and limitless conduit for all humanity to use and learn by. Although respectful of Horatio's place in theatre history, these artists have chosen to abandoned the magic mirror altogether, deciding to let it gather dust in Disney's attic. Instead of looking in on another fictional world for wisdom, they have chosen to create fictions on this side of the fissure, using fictionalized popular forms to turn our world into a place where, in every rock, one encounters an entire revealed truth. In reading this collection, one can only be left with the impression that there is still hope of creating a culture where we are all equal and where we give each other the unrelenting permission to make art for art's sake.

Re-runs and Repetition

Sarah Ruhl

1. The Era of Recycling

It seems we live in an age of cultural recycling. Re-imagined tales are everywhere, in both commercial and avant-garde re-tellings. Old movies become new musical comedies (from *Debbie Does Dallas* to *Footloose*), television shows from the seventies become new movies with the same hair-styles (*Charlie's Angels* the first and the second), Hollywood flunkies scavenge for bits of text all over the globe to pirate for the movies. Novels become movies, essays become movies, novels become plays, old novels become new novels (for instance, Michael Cunninham's *The Hours)*. So little seems to rest, sacred, in its primary form. The sonnet, at least, seems immune, until a movie producer has the guts to turn a sonnet into a treatment. Does the sonnet protect itself from genre pirates because its form is like a steel trap? That is to say, its particular content cannot live happily in another genre, unlike the novel, which is perhaps a more malleable form.

Of course, theatre has always been ripe for plot stealing—Shakespeare stole most of his plots, and Euripides re-told tales that everyone in Greece already knew. On one hand,

Americans are obsessed with originality—the new voice, the new story, and the latest artistic trend. But up against this renegade passion for the new, we live in a culture that wants stories to be recognizable, capable of being branded. Which can lead to the feeling that we are living in an era of recycling recycling? Can we distinguish the radical re-imagining of old stories from crass re-packaging? What exactly is the difference between breathing new life into an old form and repeating an old story for market value?

Within the general madness for recycling, there seems to be a particular passion right now for Greek adaptations. From Sung Rno's recent *wAve* (in which Medea becomes a Korean American housewife) to Caridad Svich's version of Iphigenia (in which the Greek landscape is transformed into a rave fable). From Chuck Mee's formidable body of work to Stephen Sondheim's *The Frogs*. I've always felt a unique energy embedded in a worthy adaptation of the Greeks, that there's something more primal going on than the general appetite for re-told stories. Maybe that's because I tried to learn ancient Greek in college and failed miserably, and I've been searching ever since for the key to its mysteries. But one might claim that the impulse to watch ancient stories over and over again is less grandly mysterious and more basic--like watching beloved re-runs on television. Maybe we just like hearing the same story over and over again. Certainly our daily lives suffer under the dread weight of formlessness. And, if that's the case, has the avant-garde lost audiences to the cultural mainstream by embracing formlessness, or put another way, abandoning formalism?

A couple of years ago, a Chinese delegation came to New York to find out more about the Broadway musical. "'We want to know how your Broadway musicals could attract such large audiences,' Mr. Yu said through a translator. 'And why our comprehensive art forms—with singing, dancing and drama—could not attract such a large audience.'... 'The audiences are aging and fewer,' said Yin Xiaodong, deputy director of the ministry's department of drama. 'We definitely see the musical, as a contemporary art form, as a way toward the rejuvenation of the ancient art forms'" ("Chinese Delegation tries to Decode Broadway's Secrets", *New York Times*, Monday, Dec. 23, 02).

The irony of a communist country looking to a capitalist country to learn more about using populism to glorify its own ancient forms is almost funny. I feel compassion for anyone looking towards the American musical as a way of revitalising ancient culture as well as ticket sales. For one thing, the American musical itself is in a crisis—beleaguered and mocked, with a diminishing ability to sell tickets and with its own lack of appeal to young, diverse audiences. The American musical itself pillages newer forms (from movies to rock songs to Bollywood to porn) in the hopes of rejuvenating itself. In an era of globalised commerce and the corporate media, one hardly knows where to look for authenticity.

2. Boredom, Comfort, and Re-runs

I recently heard a woman on *This American Life* talking about television re-runs. She was an ardent re-run fan. She explained that even if she didn't like the content of a particular show, watching it again was comforting: She said, "I don't like it. But I *know* it. I'm familiar with it. And that's enough. 80% is about comfort for me." Sound about right?

It's comforting to see familiar characters again. It's even comforting to hear familiar punch lines. The sound cue that marks scene changes in *Law and Order* is pleasing. We know it will come, and then it does, but something we don't quite know will follow. And so it returns us to a very comfortable primordial infant state. When we are infants, it's delightful to recognise our mothers. "There she is again! And again!" Teletubbies have a genius for satisfying the toddler's desire for repetition. The known is more than safe—it is primal. It is love. I recently read that we require more brain wave movement when we are asleep than when we are watching television. Think about that for a moment.

Seeing a new play doesn't give us the same moments of primal comfort that television does. We don't know the characters, we don't know the story or necessarily know the structure, and we don't know how the characters will speak. We don't know how it will all end. Instead of primal comfort, in a very good play, what we get is primal recognition. This brand of recognition puts us into contact with the present moment, rather than distancing us from it. And if the goal of art is to put us into contact with the present moment, I would argue that the dialectic between the known and the unknown helps us. The ancient stories help us, ironically, to be in contact, really in contact, with our strange contemporary moment.

Now what if we don't know Greek mythology? Not many of us are incredibly intimate with the Greeks anymore. What is the experience of seeing *Medea*, for example, without knowing she'll eventually slaughter her children? Two years ago, I saw the remarkable production of *Medea* at the Brooklyn Academy of Music, directed by

Deborah Warner. After Medea kills her children, in this production, we see the children's blood smeared across glass, and then country music comes up slowly on a radio with bad reception. Watching, I felt as though I were going to vomit. Certainly this was Aristotelian terror. I knew what was going to happen, it happened, and I was startled into nausea by a strange hybrid of the ancient and the modern—a kind of ancient inevitability up against a tinny radio with bad reception. It was in that place--between the familiar and the unfamiliar--that my gut got all riled up.

Now what if I hadn't known the story of Medea ahead of time? What if the only fact I knew before walking into the theatre was that the actress playing Medea (Fiona Shaw) was also in the Harry Potter movies playing Mrs. Dursley? What if our cultural relationship to the big, the mythic, the iconic, is now actually our relationship to Hollywood? (That modern American place where the individual becomes huge.) Then the relationship between the known and the unknown becomes *not* the relationship of old stories to new stories, but the relationship between the individual and pop culture.

I have no way of knowing what the effect of Warner's *Medea* would be on someone unfamiliar with the myth from the inside out. But I do know that I took a dear friend to the production who doesn't often go to see theatre. (Instead, she gets people off death row for a living. So she doesn't have a lot of time for theatre.) She loved the production, was very moved by it, and said, "I really loved it. But what would you say about the production if you knew about theatre? I know nothing about theatre. What would *you* say if you were talking to your theatre friends?" "I don't know," I said. "I loved it, and it was very scary." "Yes," she said, "And I thought it was very well-written," she said, "except for the choral bits. I didn't think they were so well-written." I loved that my friend (a lawyer who gets people off death row) loved *Medea* except for the badly written choral bits. She had no compunction about objecting to the choral bits, because Euripides was not, to her, sacrosanct. She responded to the play with her gut—and wondered afterwards what "qualified" people would have to say about it. Does theatre in our culture pretend to be talking to people only with special theatrical expertise? And, if so, will theatre slowly become akin to quilt making? A sweet, ancient, labor-intensive activity that's ultimately not very practical? My own love for the Greeks has nothing to do with the language of smug expertise--the audience nodding, identifying with an elite knowledge base. Instead, I'm interested in how the Greeks can refract in the gut. When my play *Eurydice* (an adaptation of the Orpheus myth told from Eurydice's point of view) was done at Madison Repertory Theatre, a number of subscribers called the box office complaining that they couldn't pronounce the play's name. And yet prior knowledge of the myth wasn't at all a prerequisite for experiencing the play in the gut. So what to do?

A dramaturg recently told me about a letter her theatre had received from a subscriber. The subscriber said, "I'm sick of seeing plays that I've seen before. And I'm also sick of seeing plays that are totally unfamiliar to me." The theatre had no choice but to throw up its hands in frustration. And yet—what if this audience member was making a deeper point? Maybe what's missing in the American theatre is a kind of primal familiarity wedded to the newness of soaring insight. After all, where do Americans receive that kind of aesthetic joy today?

Church, pop music, television and movies. Church follows a rigid familiar structure with some variation. Rock music, television, and movies also follow a rigid form. Songs on the radio follow a rigid pattern of chorus and verse. Movies have plot points on page thirty, sixty, and ninety. A television show is even more rigid, requiring turning points at each commercial break. Even "alternative rock" and "independent movies" follow this form. The market simply does not tolerate formlessness.

Do music, television and film producers enforce rigid forms in order to insure mass sales? Are they underestimating their audiences? Or does mass culture actually respond to the rigidity of form because we are pleased in a primal way by the combination of the surprise inside the familiar? That is to say: The unknown candy inside the known piñata.

3. Reproduction or Repetition

My teacher, Paula Vogel, is a consummate populist and also a renegade experimenter with form. She reinvents form in every play that she writes. In her most recent play, *The Long Christmas Ride Home,* she tells the story of a modern family through the form of Bunraku puppets. The play follows one family's shattering Christmas dinner. The play is told in narrative form, with three children sitting in the back of a family car as the father drives to and from a terrible Christmas dinner. Each child manipulates a puppet representing them, and the puppets become as real, in some ways more real, than the children, in the re-enacting of their memories do. Vogel references Thornton Wilder's one act play *The Long Christmas Dinner,* in which Genevieve says, "I shall never marry, Mother—I shall sit in this house beside you forever, as though life were one long happy Christmas dinner." In contrast, in Vogel's play, none of the children marry happily, as though marked irrevocably by one very long Christmas dinner. They return again and again to the Christmas dinner the way we return, with striking repetition, to the site of a wound. Vogel simultaneously alludes to Wilder's experimentation with form (*The Long Christmas Dinner* traverses ninety years and ninety Christmas dinners in less than thirty pages) and Eastern theatrical traditions. The ghost of a brother in *The Long Christmas Ride Home* returns through a formal dance in ancient Noh tradition. The Bunraku puppets are part of an ancient Japanese form, and, in a sense, they are familiar to everyone's collective unconscious. (If you believe in the collective unconscious.) But the puppets are unfamiliar to most contemporary Western theatregoers. And so, when we watch the puppets stand in for the people in *The Long Christmas Ride Home,* we feel mesmerised by how alien they are as objects and how unusual they seem in the theatre, but also how human, how familiar, how child-like they feel. The puppets remind us of how distanced these children are from their own experience. And yet their distancing effect pulls us deeply towards an in-between space—the place between knowing and not knowing, the present and the past. I believe that it is inside this space between the unknown and the known, the ancient and the modern, that the invisible life occurs on stage.

Paula Vogel contends that form is intimately related to memory, and that theatre making is a form of memory making. She says, "Where and what do we remember? And the only way to forget, paradoxically, is to expose your devices and keep them in front of everybody because through repetition you can make us all forget. We take it for granted and stop looking at it. So then you can make us re-remember" (Paula Vogel, the Playwright's Voice, edited by David Saran, 271).

To re-remember...to remember again. Not nostalgia, but a deeper form of remembering, a structure of loss. What I believe she is getting at is the revelation of some kind of *being*. And conversely, what re-runs and industrial recycling diminish, in my opinion, is the evocation of being. It seems that one form of aesthetic repetition can enhance being, and the other does the opposite—it deadens. Walter Benjamin, the philosopher and cultural theorist remarkably anticipated the difference between spiritual repetition and mechanical reproduction. Benjamin all but predicted reality television, digital sampling, and e-mail, even though he died in 1940. He understood where we were headed. He argues that what is missing in the reproduced art form is the "aura" or authenticity of the object. He writes:

> "That which withers in the age of mechanical reproduction is the aura of the work of art...One might generalise by saying: the technique of reproduction detaches the reproduced object from the domain of tradition. By making many reproductions it substitutes a plurality of copies for a unique existence."(Illuminations, "The Work of Art in the Age of Mechanical Reproduction, 221).

Benjamin understood that, in the world we would live in, very little would be unique, un-reproducible. I grew up with the mimeograph. Now I open my laptop—there I see iTunes, iphoto, and idvd—every personal literary artifact—every beloved song or photograph—memory itself--can be reproduced digitally. A click of the button and these artifacts can be circulated. It's certainly a convenient means of reproduction. But what is lost?

If it were, as Benjamin argues, *the aura* that is lost in the age of mechanical reproduction, I would argue that it is precisely this aura that *repetition* tries to reclaim. That is to say, when we re-tell an ancient story, we repeat the story without reproducing it exactly. Theatre in general is a medium of live repetition rather than mechanical reproduction. An actor biologically *cannot repeat* a performance, even though they perform the same play night after night. An exact reproduction would be not only undesirable, but also impossible. And so it is that when we tell a tale over again, it changes, never static. What child has not thrilled in asking a parent to re-tell a childhood story over and over again? The story changes slightly every night but leaves a primal mark through repetition. That's a different sort of comfort from the comfort we get watching re-runs, because the re-run is exactly reproduced, rather than repeated. Spiritual practices all involve repetition and variation—daily prayers, weekly communion, fasting, and holy days. With repetition of the outward form, the inner value reveals itself and, one hopes, changes for the better.

Theatre, then, becomes a radical spiritual form in our age of mechanical reproduction, because it is a form of repetition very difficult to sell. It's impossible to sell the oral tradition. It changes as we tell it. You can't record it. A videotape of a theatrical performance is always terrible—it never conveys atmosphere, which is the life-blood of theatre, so the reproduction feels limp, almost grotesque. All we can actually *own* of our experience in the theatre is a ticket stub—a souvenir—quite literally, a remembrance.

As our culture moves more and more towards exact biological and digital reproductions—cloning and its aftermath--it is left for artists to search for that which cannot be exactly reproduced. Re-runs give us a false sense of our own immortality—Meredith Baxter Burney will always say her lines the same way on *Family Ties*—she will never age. An irreproducible piece of art, by contrast, makes us aware of our own fragility. Both re-runs and repetition comment on our inevitable decline—but do we want numb comfort in the face of our mortality, or do we prefer the white heat of the present moment?

The difference between re-runs and repetition is brilliantly invoked by the musician Gil Scott-Heron who sang in 1974:

"The revolution will not be televised,
will not be televised
will not be televised, will not be televised.
The revolution will be no re-run brothers--
The revolution will be live."

The death of reproduction is proclaimed through the repetition of the live voice: "will not be televised, will not be televised, will not be televised". Here is the difference between repetition as mantra, as call to arms, as invocation to live being—and re-runs as a lulling, deadening force. He calls for a live revolution in real time. In our time, when the digital age has re-defined grass-roots political movements, when everything is branded, when, in fact, the revolution *appears to have been televised*—anything the artist can make to resist reproduction, to bring *live people into one room together,* is an act of resistance.

Working towards new forms and towards the memory of old forms is a process without calculation. For artists who conjure the historic and contemporary invisible, for artists who make a thing that is essentially incapable of being owned, for artists who experiment with wild fancy and then invite *everyone* to the table to partake—to you I give my undying loyalty and love.

Big dreams:

An Interview with Eugenio Barba

Dijana Milosevic

[Eugenio Barba is the director and the founder of Odin Teatret-the Nordic Theatre Laboratory an international theatre group based in Holstebro, Denmark. He is also the director of ISTA- International School of Theatre Anthropology, a prominent theatre theoretician and the author of many books and essays. Eugenio Barba and his theatre represent a major reference point in contemporary theatre. Formed in 1964 Odin Teatret's work was characterised initially by exceptionally rigorous training and one-to-two year rehearsal periods toward the development of a single production, which would be seen by sixty or seventy spectators. The group intentionally designed productions for an audience that could fit into their workroom. In 1974, Odin Teatret moved to a village in southern Italy to continue developing their 'secret' theatre only to discover that the intense quality of secrecy that they had forged from 1964-74 had created an insular group and work mentality. Thereafter, Barba and his company sought to alter the atmosphere of secrecy and engage with communities directly, whilst maintaining the core group model, in an effort to make theatre that was an instrument for social-spiritual change. What is radical and politically driven about Barba's work is often overlooked because of the extremely limited ways in which the word 'radical' is used. This is unfortunate because Barba's delicately insistent, organic approach to re-defining the meaning, for example, of what a 'reservation, ghetto or pueblo' is has had a major impact on communities and theatre ensembles working in Latin America, the Caribbean and elsewhere. As consistent marginalisation in language and deed affects émigrés and displaced peoples the world over, Barba's dedication to his Third Theatre is a living, radical reminder of the power of reclamation, and of sustaining a non-market-driven ensemble in an increasingly greed-driven, corporately-geared global society. For Barba, the Other voice is the point of intersection and exchange. His search for signs hidden on the cultural surface – and this includes the living culture of the core group of Odin Teatret itself – is evidence of his desire to see history anew through older as well as shifting orders of meaning.

Dijana Milosevic is one of the founders and director of DAH Theatre in Belgrade, Serbia. DAH's work began on the streets of

Belgrade performing discreet actions of unusually private, vulnerable protest-theatre. The company has evolved over the years toward working in conventional and unconventional spaces alike, but throughout all their work runs a constant commitment to investigating the historicity of time and its relationship to memory. Usually devising pieces from within or through collaboration with artists and musicians from outside Serbia, DAH, led by Milosevic as its artistic director, creates strong yet fragile pieces that focus on ritualised gesture and action and which are often centred on the female body as recorder of memory. This interview took place on 1 October 2004 at Odin Theatre in Holstebro, Denmark on the celebration of the Odin Teatret's 40th anniversary. It was originally conducted in English. Corrections (for clarity and grammar) to the text were made by US playwright-librettist and DAH collaborator Ruth Margraff. However, an effort has been made, in keeping with this volume's democratic approach to acknowledging the social, linguistic and historical boundaries often placed on speech types and languages and thereby the norms governing them, to privilege both artists' relationship, as non-native speakers, to English as a 'foreign' language. –Caridad Svich]

DM: Forty years is an impressive amount of time for a theatre group to be together. How do you account for your longevity?
EB: It's surprising that a core of actors has been together for so long. There are many positive aspects to this: the fact that we know each other; that we have a common vocabulary and profound understanding of each other; that we have a common artistic biography; and that we have shared so many dreams and struggles over such a long period of time. The negative side to this is that we know each other so well that over the years we have created 'a personal identity.' A routine has developed and solidified itself. This happens with all groups and institutions. It is an essential part of a group's formation. However, it is important to create antibodies to this routine, so the group can survive and be healthy from within. The routine should be the pillar, which supports the structure. Creating a space for viruses (and I mean this in the positive sense) allows for change to occur, and thus, for evolution. When a crisis comes up, or a situation arises which is outside the routine, then, the group can face it. It is a healthy organism. It is this dynamic, this dialectic, between preserving and maintaining who we are and at the same time trying to change that has kept us going for forty years. We are constantly mediating between the collective tasks and aims of the group as a

whole, and the personal needs of each individual.

DM: For a long time you did not take in new company members, but now, you have younger actors in the company. It must make quite a difference.

EB: It's very different. I have been training my actors for years from early in the morning to late in the evening. I would train them for three-five years, and then send them out into the world

Many of these actors are still with Odin. It is difficult for me now to spend so many hours exclusively on training because Odin has so many other activities. We have international tours and the International School for Theatre Anthropology, and all this comparative research in performative traditions and styles from cultures other than European. So, I have not been working with young actors for many, many years. Members of the company, though, have been training, and being in some cases economically responsible for, young people, some of whom have ended up as members of the company. Julia Varley is one of these actors, and now she has been with the company for twenty-five years! There are also young people who simply train with us, but they are not members of Odin. We call them "laborants" which means that they learn how to work in a laboratory setting, but their task is

just to learn.
DM: When you founded your theatre in 1964, did you have a vision that it would be around for forty years?
EB: When you are young, you don't think about getting old. When you are young, you just fight to keep your head above water, to survive, and try to achieve the most basic things in theatre: how to acquire knowledge, and achieve recognition; how to build a network of contacts and get a space to develop and present your work; how to create a true environment within a company and how to be able to function as a theatre company. If you had asked me then what the future would be like, I wouldn't have said it would be like this. On the one hand you have to build something very solid, which we can call a 'superstition,' which is what keeps individuals working together. You can also use a more noble word like 'values'. I call it 'superstition' because for me the word goes beyond my personally limited biographical needs. Even if you build something solid, you still have to create elements of challenge, surprise, and enthusiasm in your collaborators because these elements are what keep people together and engaged in action, especially when they are working without the guarantee of money and security that institutions can usually offer artists. Odin's actors live on minimum wage.

After so many years of working, they have seen so many things, and been spiritually rewarded in so many different ways from doing the work, but it is a profession that tears at you nevertheless, so, how to keep the fire lit? That is the constant question.
DM: You often write about the social mission of the theatre. And what is the mission of Odin Theatre today in relation to society?
EB: Each theatre should build its own superstition, its own identity, which always means to face the "polis", the context, that very specific context in which theatre exists. You cannot speak about a theatre's mission or social function in general terms. Odin theatre is a group of foreigners who not even speak the language of the country in which we are working! We have been learning this language but we still speak with an accent. So, we are excluded often from using texts, because it would not be appropriate and indeed rather grotesque if an actor is reciting a very tragic, pathetic monologue with a heavy accent and no diction! Therefore we have had to invent a different way of telling stories in our theatre, and we have done so through presence, through emphasising our presence. This is what Odin theatre has had to do. So, the question becomes 'how to be a foreigner?' How to exploit the disadvantages and advantages that come with being 'a foreigner"

and how to transform them? Not into something bizarre or interesting, but rather the opposite: where foreigners can keep their particular nature - who they are and where they are from - and at the same time be part of the integrated dynamic of the "polis", of the society. I would say that this is what Odin Teatret has been doing for many years and I think we are succeeding in Holstebro, in Denmark, where there are so many xenophobic tendencies. We have been able to not only be accepted in Holstebro but also somehow make people feel proud that their theatre is so strange, and made by foreigners!
DM: In performances, and I've seen almost all your performances, if not live then on video, I have found that you are obsessed with history: with the past and contemporary history. Your performances are also very political, although never in direct way.
EB: To paraphrase Napoleon: the destiny of human beings in the future will be politics. When we speak about history we have to think of two different things. First there is personal history (your biography, the place where you live, the family you come from, your environment, the beliefs you were given, the social conditions in which you grew up, what are you rejecting, what you want to escape from). Let's call this, then, 'little history.' And then there is big history with a capital H,

which is what is happening around us, and much of big history we often feel we don't understand. Big History is an almost blind force that can feel quite sudden and cruel, like a cyclone, which just destroys and upsets everything. So how to make little history survive, and not only survive but not be crushed by big history? This obsesses me personally and in my work.

I come from a family where all the men died in the Second World War. My father died in the Second World War and all my uncles too. I grew up in a family, then, where all the women were dressed in black and living without men. And what was interesting- of course not amusing, but interesting- was that some of the men were fighting on the fascist side. Others were on the antifascist side, which was a typical split in my family. When I left Italy, I became an emigrant. I experienced what it means to be a foreigner working abroad who faces xenophobia and rejection daily, but also great generosity and great solidarity too in Norway and afterwards in Denmark. So, I try to protect my little history, because it is important for my own integrity, and my own completeness as a human being; I do not want my little history to be violated by outside expectations and prejudices. There is a mental image, a stereotype other people have when they meet an Italian and one who comes from the southern part of Italy. It is a stereotype that has become an archetype. Therefore I understand that part of creating a performance has to do with acknowledging that this archetype exists and that it is recognised by every spectator in one way or another because the archetype has become part of our historical awareness.

DM: Through your work, you have inspired many people and spurred the formation of many groups. Many people consider you and Odin Theatre actors as their master. What do you think is the responsibility of the master towards the pupil?

EB: We choose our masters in the sense that we use certain individuals and certain experiences as a point of reference not to imitate them, because you cannot imitate them, but to supersede them, to let ourselves be inspired, to be better than our fathers. Other people call me master. I don't consider them my pupils. I don't think that an artist has children or heirs. Many people can be inspired but inspiration means that you have to change. What inspires you must be transformed into what is meaningful to you and your culture. In this sense I know that Odin Theatre has contributed to the practice, and I am happy when I cannot recognise my inspiration on others. Responsibility exists. We know that Odin is a lonely star from which many theatre groups, especially young ones, try to find their way. But I can't think about this. I can only think about the importance of the last stage of a career- of how to die. Because at the end death decides, just like the final act of a tragedy decides the nature of the whole structure and plot of the play.

DM: You invented the term 'third theatre.' I guess your association was the term Third World?

EB: Yes, it was during the BITEF Festival in Belgrade; at the same time there was Theatre of Nations in 1976 and I was given the possibility of organising a meeting of many theatre groups. I was thinking about the double face of theatre - one was so-called traditional theatre and one opposing this tradition we used to call the avant-garde. But in the 1970s I was discovering many other manifestations of theatrical expression that were very different. They had none of this sort of identity in terms of genre. So, I called it 'third theatre.' These groups that belonged to this theatre were the poor ones, the discriminated ones, those who were not taken in consideration by critics or theatre historians. They were not being regarded with interest, even though these groups had more spectators sometimes than the old institutional theatres in a country. Also, in many countries in Latin America, where we toured, there wasn't a so-called traditional theatre in the European mode. This theatre I was witness to was just a new sort of life. It was a destabilising force. But this force did not only represent something bright and creative, it also contained destructive elements. So, within this third theatre, there was and is a huge universe, which is not defined by esthetics, visions, ideology, or techniques. It can have a wide range of political and formal manifestations. In all of these manifestations, however, you see fragility. There is the urge to break boundaries, but at the same time this very urge makes groups and projects appear and dissolve like snow in the sun. Their life span can be very short.

DM: And what do you think is the situation of the "third theatre" today?

EB: The world today is different from the world when we gathered at the theatre conference in Belgrade in 1976. At the same time a new generation of young people comes to the theatre and sees it as a no- man's land where they can free themselves from certain obligations and ways of thinking. It is a no-man's land where they can find their own role in society, their own mission, whether it be through not accepting the political ideas of their own country or integrating themselves in the foreign county. So, this no-man's land is an island of dissidents. In this land live those who don't share the common ideas, superstitions and values of the people around them, but at the same time they are able to establish the praxis of how they can live by doing so through making art. Theatre can represent this island of freedom. It can represent this island of dissidents even in the heart of the civilised world, whether it is in big cities or small villages.

DM: What do you think is society's responsibility towards a theatre group?

EB: What is society? People in power? They change. In most so-called democratic countries, they change. In certain countries there is this superstition that culture should be protected because it expresses the national values of the people. Therefore, certain kinds of theatre are looked upon as treasures and museums are built. And then, there are other kinds of artistic expression that perhaps people in power cannot recognise as national expression, or artistic expression, because originality and artistic difference are not considered valuable commodities. There are other countries that are full of creativity and initiative like USA and Japan and they don't even have a Ministry of Culture to give theatre groups money! The whole of Europe is giving less and less money to artists. Is this the responsibility of society towards artists? I do not think so. I also do not think artists have a responsibility towards society. What does 'society' mean? Society means many different kinds of people. What does it mean then- to be responsible towards the xenophobes, to the 25 % of xenophobes in Denmark- do I have a responsibility towards them? I can try to live and do my craft in such a manner that I will earn society's respect, but to feel responsibility? I do not understand what that means.

DM: Once I asked you, I think it was ten years ago, 'what do you think makes young groups grow?' and you answered 'big dreams.' Do you still think that? What would you say to young theatre groups?

EB: When I said 'big dreams' it meant that you must have superstition. Superstition is something that is much bigger then you. It can be your love for someone - your mother for instance - and so you become an actor, or you are very fond of Artaud and take a certain creative path, etc. When we speak about dreams it means that we have to let that part of ourselves, which lives in exile, to be liberated in a very indirect way through this craft which we call theatre. The expression of this dream manifests itself as if it were a wild dog. Not a domesticated dog. For there is the theatre that is domesticated and meets the criteria and expectations of society and the theatre scene, and there is another theatre, where you just follow a separate, other path. The former kind of theatre demands much more of artists because they have to comply with expectations. But in the end you still need a superstition, as I like to call it. It could be a big dream. It could be your faith that theatre can change the world, or that theatre can change who you are, or that it can give you the possibility of approaching another realm of reality. The dream has to go beyond the ephemeral time of performance, for it begins after the performance is over. It is like putting a virus in the systems of your spectators. They don't have to know that this virus is coming from your performance. But as they witness the work they are receiving another intellectual, emotional metabolism into their organisms. This is how you can contribute, maybe, to a different way of seeing.

Off the Map:

Charting an American Theatre of Place

Todd London

The Stage Manager, you remember, welcomes us into Grover's Corners with exquisite specificity. He points out all the churches -- each denomination -- town hall, the post office and jail, a row of stores, schools, houses, down to the burdock in Mrs. Gibbs' garden and to the butternut tree "Right here." "Polish Town's across the tracks," he tells us, as if it occurs to him that someone might someday write Their Town about the marginalised Poles. By the end of Act I, Thornton Wilder, the playwright behind this tour, connects this pinpoint locale with a universe beyond imagining. We hear tell of a letter addressed: "Jane Crofut; The Crofut Farm; Grover's Corners; Sutton County; New Hampshire; United States of America; Continent of North America; Western Hemisphere; the Earth; the Solar System; the Universe; the Mind of God." From a single soul on a tiny plot of land to the mind of god....

Works of theatre take aim like the address on Jane Crofut's letter: They begin with a small circle on a map -- the one the characters and, possibly, the audience inhabit -- cross time and space, linking us as they go, guiding our awareness toward the connective mysteries of creation. Ideally, like the letter, they reach their destination.

All theatre is local. The Greeks knew it, as did the Elizabethans, the U.S. frontier troupers, the Dadaists, and artists of almost every epoch in theatrical history. Only 20th-century America seems regularly to forget, in the hunger to mass market art, to move it, to reach the greatest numbers. As a result, we exist in a state of perpetual tension between the local and the national, the regional and the Centre.

It would be nice to believe that this tension -- specifically between Broadway and the theatre of America's other cities and towns -- was a dead issue. It's not. Broadway forever doubles as artistic black hole and a radiating centre of the English-speaking theatre. Less than a decade ago, an exhibit at The Museum of the City of New York, called "Broadway: The History of the American Theatre," defined out of existence all nonmusical, non-Broadway theatre with a single "the." Ethel Merman had a wall and Rodgers & Hammerstein had a corner; others, from Le Gallienne to Le Mamet, not a mention. Provincetown, San Francisco and Kentucky -- all blown off the face of the theatrical-historical map by a 10-square-block piece of real estate.

Meanwhile, the influential movement to "decentralise" the theatre, now a half-century old, remains chronically schizoid: Is it regional (referring to place), resident (because it provides homes for artists), or Broadway bound? Is our nation's theatre centrifugal -- perpetually in flight from New York -- or centripetal -- constantly headed back? Argue the preeminence of non-New York theatre (even to educated theatregoers) without using the Great White Centre as your reference point. It can't be done. "You see, *Angels in America* began there and there....Wendy Wasserstein premiered her Tony-winning plays over there...August Wilson? Connect the dots." In 2003, Nilo Cruz's *Anna in the Tropics* stunned insiders by winning a Pulitzer Prize when only Miami audiences had seen it. Almost immediately, skeptics began questioning its value by asking, "Yes, but, how will it do on Broadway?" It didn't do well. The Prize's prestige didn't carry any more weight than it had eleven years earlier when Robert Schenkkan's *The Kentucky Cycle* became the first non-New York play to be Pulitzered and then pummeled by the big city press. Even today, New York, specifically Broadway, is the final validator.

From its beginnings, the regional theatre sought out, but out is where it never quite got.

What will it take to cut the cord that keeps Chicago, New Haven, L.A. tied to the mythical middle of midtown Manhattan?

What it will take, what it has taken, is a different idea of theatre, one that's been crystallising over the past 10 or 15 years away from traditional centres of the art. A new breed of artists, more far-flung and unassuming, has broken the centrifugal-centripetal deadlock, not by forcing it but by walking away. A coincidence of era, the will to diversity, and a hardening of American theatrical arteries has propelled numerous theatre artists to the most unlikely spots: rural byroads, urban housing projects, quiet towns, and communities in crisis. They've staked out Grover's Corners and Polish Town across the tracks. On their way they're creating something truly radical and more uniquely American than the European-modelled institutional theatres: a professional, activist, community theatre of place.

It's called Jewish Geography, but you don't have to be Jewish to play. I learned the game at college in Protestant Iowa, surrounded by other Jews from Long Island, New Jersey, and the north shore of Chicago. Elsewhere, though, it's played by African Americans, Mennonites, and French semioticians. The game consists of two questions: 1) "Where are you from?" followed by, 2) "Do you know _____? The blank is filled in with the name of someone else the questioner knows from the town or community identified in the answer to number one. The point of the game is to create instant community. By establishing shared knowledge of a place, you can find people you have in common. By discovering common ties, you connect yourself to new people in a new, shared place.

Theatrical events follow the same course. They move from place, common ground, to the people inhabiting it. Performers and audiences occupy the same room in a particular place on the globe. From Illyria to the South Pacific, however exotic the setting, the actual location of the play is always *here*. Beginning in the mid-'80s, "site-specific" theatres, such as New York's En Garde Arts and the Hillsborough Moving Company of Tampa capitalised on this fact by commissioning theatrical work for nontheatrical -- "found" -- spaces: hotels, parks, docks, abandoned buildings in splendid decay. Watching these "pieces", we participate not in the conventions of the stage but in the fact of a singular place. Likewise, Environmental theatres of the '60s, such as Richard Schechner's Performance Groups, revised the performer-spectator relationship by reinventing, with each production, the architecture of the theatre.

Even classics, which survive by universal appeal, start place specific. When Wilder set out to boil the theatre down to its essentials, as a way of probing the painful, transitory beauty of everyday life, he hit upon a bare stage, actors as actors, and the details of place. Moliere's another kind of example, three centuries away. We can laugh with recognition at the type of miser, misanthrope or religious hypocrite he sketches, but when he wrote the plays he often had actual people in mind, many of whom were sitting in the audience, vying for a seat near King Louis. Most everybody watching knew everybody else. Sometimes the guy who thought he was being lampooned gave himself away by writing a furious letter of protest to the King. Sometimes, if the joke's butt was another actor, he'd stage his own counterattack -- a re*butt*al. It was local satire, interclaque attack.

America's current theatre of place is an often-activist, community-based art that dreams globally and acts locally. It belongs not to regions or centres but to specific, square-yard-by-square-yard pieces of turf. If "decentralization" was a battle cry for the regional theatre, "recentralization" might be a motto for the new pioneers: to re-centre the American theatre in neighborhoods and communities, from fishing villages of the West to the Main Streets of Pennsylvania to the Flatbush section of Brooklyn. The lure or repulsion of Broadway doesn't enter into it; sometimes, what we usually think of as theatre doesn't either. Because it builds on the singularity of a where, no two artists or groups are alike. This makes defining a "movement" slippery. The shapes change the means vary, but the primary ends remain the same: to foster community within an established place.

Some troupes seem fairly conventional, except for a devotion to their hometowns unthinkable for urban institutional theatres. The Bloomsburg Theatre Ensemble in rural Pennsylvania, for example, offers up a standard nonprofit repertoire in an area that, with a population near 12,000, should never be able to sustain a professional company; moreover, ensemble members are as intimately involved with the town's governance and economic struggles (the sustenance of a viable downtown, for instance) as they are with its cultural life. "It's the regional theatre goal cubed," a company member explained when I visited BTE, "not just a theatre in every major city, but one in each community." The tiny outposts of Northern California have been home to no fewer than 10 permanent theatre companies (including the improbably long-lived Dell 'Arte Players in Blue Lake), back-to-the-land radicals with a taste for political satire and a survivalist dependence on their neighbors.

The roots of these companies are deep, not just geographically but historically as well. It's arguable that the first art theatres in America were, in fact, theatres of place, from the Little Theatre of Chicago (1912), the Toy Theatre of Boston (1912), and the Wisconsin Dramatic Society (1911), to university-based companies like the North Dakota and Carolina Playmakers. Even further back, art theatres began as part of the process of American assimilation and immigrant community-building through settlement houses, like Chicago's Hull House and New York's Henry Street Settlement, home to the renowned Neighborhood Playhouse.

Other contemporary artists gather material from actual places without settling in them. At the height of the solo performance boom in the '90s, confessional storytelling co-existed with more journalistic work. *Some People*, for example, Danny Hoch's one-man cavalcade of Brooklyn characters, provoked audiences to listen to the distinct strains of language and dialect that make up the five-borough Babel. His linguistic mimicry was precisely geographical, an artistic map of his street corner of the world. One of America's most original and successful solo performers,

Anna Deavere Smith, began by culling material from women she met on the road, before setting her sights on the citizens of racially divided neighborhoods like Crown Heights, Brooklyn and South Central, L.A. She interviewed and taped her subjects, and then incisively impersonated them on stage, in their own words. Both these soloists created, and continue to create, personal/political landscapes, mapping the American present as they went.

What further sets this late-20th-century avant-garde apart from the movement that brought art-theatre to mainland America is its insistence that the *process* of theatre, as much as the product, is integral to the nation's daily life, wherever it's lived. Fighting a national drift towards unconnectedness, these artists dig their heels into the soil of established communities, either for extended stays or for good. Professional artists work with, not just for, audiences and amateurs. When the Cornerstone Theatre Company revises classic plays with folks from Watts, the Santa Monica malls, or the Chinatown of L.A., where the company settled several years ago after its itinerant beginnings, a sense of shared place animates the final product. In its earliest work with the citizens of Marfa, Texas or Port Gibson, Mississippi, the company helped

transform the landscape as well, by leaving newly formed theatres behind.
Sometime the theatre of place begins with the lore of a spot on the map. In Colquitt, Georgia, insiders and outsiders, pros and locals, have set in motion an ongoing, evolving oral-history--pure place; I saw a similar shared history enacted in an old barn by descendants of a Mennonite colony in Newport News, Virginia. The polymorphous American Festival Project, which began in 1982 as a cultural exchange between the African-American Junebug Productions from New Orleans and Appalachia's Roadside Theater now includes more than a dozen dance and theatre companies, such as Urban Bush Women, El Teatro de la Esperanza, Robbie McCauley and Company, and A Traveling Jewish Theatre. All or some of the project's companies offer joint workshops, performances and full-scale festivals during residencies ranging from weeks to years in communities as disparate as Maine, Miami, and Montana. Twenty-one such festivals in nineteen states have promoted exchanges between the culture of art and that of daily, rooted life.

Because so much of this theatre of place has evolved from the issue-oriented theatres of the 60s and 70s -- The Free Southern Theatre and El Teatro Campesino, to name two -- it often mingles aesthetics with activism. As a result, these troupes are sometimes accused of mistaking social work for art. They lead with their social consciences and draw on models of social outreach, civil rights demonstration, and grassroots organising, and political theatre as they try to activate healing in tribe-torn America. The Living Stage Theatre at Washington, D.C.'s Arena Stage, for many years one of the nation's largest activist theatres, ran workshops in schools, prisons, community centres -- wherever there were lives to save through art -- and created heart-stoppingly vital theatre with actors and non-. John Malpede's Los Angeles Poverty Department began working with homeless people in 1985, cobbling together shows one critic called "bizarre, unpredictable, emotionally supercharged affairs that walk a fine line between stark raving madness and frightening clarity."

All this activity comprises what Gerry Givnish, director of Painted Bride Arts Centre in Philadelphia, once called "a giving back" by building community locally. Clearly, the giving goes both ways. Theatre artists share dramatic techniques and expertise and, so, help communities theatricalise their stories and play out crises within. The communities give back a sense of purpose, connectedness, and, of course, the stories themselves. They give artists a place.

This spiritual dimension, sometimes obscured by the work's stark political content, runs deep and -- democratic, populist, and good-neighbor-transcendental -- feels deeply American. Its motto might be taken from Emerson, who, in his journal writes: *"The place which I have not sought, but in which my duty places me, is a sort of royal palace. If I am faithful to it, I move in it with a pleasing awe at the immensity of the chain of which I hold the last link in my hand and am led by it...."*

* * *

The professional, regional theatre and the professional, community theatre of place were separated at birth. Like so many extraordinary ideas, they seem to have sprung full-blown from the visionary brain of Hallie Flanagan, director of the Works Progress Administration's Federal Theatre Project. Begun in 1935 as a relief -- read "jobs" -- program and killed by an Act of Congress four years later, Flanagan's project anticipated everything that came after (including ongoing trouble with the Feds). "Part of a tremendous re-thinking, re-building, and re-dreaming of America," as she called it, FTP would radiate over the vast geography of America by creating a "federation of theatres" subsidised nationally but administered locally. They'd spring up in all shapes and sizes: new play theatres, classical ones, circuses, puppet shows. Metropolitan resident companies would tour regional circuits of small theatres and work with local groups to develop regional playwrights.

Flanagan envisaged her experimental, pioneer, populist theatre interacting with -- feeding into -- the commercial, Broadway theatre, and so she enlisted the talents of Broadway artists like Elmer Rice, John Houseman, and the very young Orson Welles. She also saw it leaving Broadway behind. Local work by local artists -- a true theatre of place -- would become part of the fabric of American life. Oklahoma got a theatre for the blind in which students from the school for the blind worked as actors from scripts transcribed in Braille. A unit in Omaha played to audiences, 90% of which had never seen a live show. (Afterward, the story goes, Flanagan watched audiences wait to touch the actors to confirm that they were "real people.") On Oct. 27, 1936, Sinclair Lewis's <u>It Can't Happen Here</u> opened simultaneously in 21 American cities.

With labor and construction funds from the WPA, America's longest lived and most imitated place-based theatre -- Paul Green's local-historical drama, The Lost Colony, in North Carolina -- began its perpetual, perennial life.

After FTP's demise, one branch of Flanagan's revolution sprouted at a time. First, a decade later, the regional theatre movement began, resembling her metropolitan resident companies. Soon after, professional activity took root in America's smaller communities -- a theatre of place. Both branches struggle for validation: one against the idea of New York's centrifugal power; the other, against the notion that quality art and outreach don't mix. Flanagan fought these battles, too. That's partially why she forged connections with theatre luminaries where she could; she had to prove that her enterprise was real theatre: that talented artists did, in fact, wind up on relief rolls.

As Flanagan made clear, powerful art can and does happen anywhere, for all sorts of alchemical reasons. It succeeds when it effectively confirms or challenges a community's idea about itself. When it continues to do so over time, it lasts. (Ezra Pound put it best: "Literature is news that *stays* news.") It's too early to know what the implications of this renewed activity are for the future. Will it forever change the way theatre fits into American life? Will it foster real community or false art? Will it fall out of the arts altogether, until it seems a subsystem of grassroots social service? Will it save the arts from universal defunding -- by being nonelitist and a justifiable contributor to down-home America -- or prove too subversive for fainthearts with money to spend? Will criticism -- which in reaction to a true theatre of place means something more like cartography -- learn a language that goes beyond "universal" quality to one of purpose and context and local value?

When the citizens of Grover's Corners plan their time capsule, they choose to include copies of both *The New York Times* ("Of course," the Stage Manager shrugs) and Mr. Webb's *Sentinel*, the town paper. As a final object for future interest, the Stage Manager decides to include a copy of the play itself, so "the people a thousand years from now will know a few simple facts about us...." However the American theatre of place looks to our critical eyes in ten years or in that distant moment when the Grover's Corners time capsule gets opened, it's here now. Right here.

Can old forms be reinvigorated?" Radical Populism and New Writing in British theatre

Aleks Sierz

At the start of Gregory Burke's award-winning *Gagarin Way* (first performed at Edinburgh's Traverse Theatre in 2001), one of the characters says: "There's nothing the general public likes better than a vicarious wander through the world ay the full-time criminal." He is talking about the popularity, among French intellectuals, of Jean Genet – "every criminal worth his salt had tay have a literary sideline" – but the phenomenon is a much more general one. (1) It's now called "cultural tourism", and it's not new. John McGrath, writing about the first new wave of British postwar drama, put it like this: "This famed New Era/Dawn/Direction of British theatre was no more than the elaboration of a theatrical technique for turning authentic working-class experience into satisfying thrills for the bourgeoisie." (2) Clearly, new writing has from the start been coloured by notions of radicalism, populism and authenticity. Ever since George Devine's stewardship of the Royal Court, and the work of Joan Littlewood at Stratford East, it is easy to see why ideas about radical populism – the legacy of Littlewood and McGrath – have had such an emotional pull on British theatre workers. After all, since the mid-1960s many in the profession have been liberal leftists, attracted by the idea that what they were doing was not only artistic but radical too. It is also clear that, in the wake of 9/11, such inspirational traditions have not been forgotten. For example, on 7 March 2003, London's Red Room theatre company held an event called Going Public, which explored new writing as a public forum. In its publicity leaflet, the company asked: "Can old forms be reinvigorated? Are there new forms that we're ignoring? Might the recent deaths of John McGrath and Joan Littlewood inspire new thinking about popular forms?" (3) So what has happened to these aspirations? To find out, I talked to some of the main players in the British new writing scene.

The past: "something from another era"

The bad news is that, in British theatre today, the words "radical populism" immediately conjure up images from the past rather than activity in the present. Paul Sirett is typical in saying that they remind him of "The Living Newspaper and Theatre Workshop, Joan Littlewood and John McGrath." (4) He also points out that, at the Royal Court, George Devine staged John Arden because he believed in his work, even though it did very badly at the box office, while he staged Arnold Wesker, whose work he didn't like, because it brought in a popular audience. The concept of access is clearly central to any discussion of radical populism. Graham Whybrow agrees that the idea of radical populism is "something from another era":

> "The terminology comes from writers seeking to make a political intervention through the arts, and therefore keen to reach a wider audience by embracing a broad aesthetic so that they are not cornered into artistic coteries, which they despise. It's a workerist, or Trotskyist mentality: you break into the system in order to change more people. Rather than writing a play for a fringe theatre, you write a drama for television. The 1960s generation of David Mercer, Dennis Potter and Trevor Griffiths was interested in radical populism and keen to speak to as many people as possible. Today, this pairing of popular form and radical content is rare because the ideology underpinning that idea has been cast into doubt. Writers have a more simple artistic dilemma of whether they want to reach a coterie, by narrowcasting, or broadcast in a more popular medium."

But not every voice consigns radical populism to the past. Roxana Silbert argues that "it is theatre which is popular in form and radical in content (questioning, oppositional, challenging, transgressive). It also makes me think of playwrights who've consciously chosen to write or use popular forms in order to change society: Dario Fo, Joan Littlewood and John McGrath." She points out that the political plays of the late 1970s and 1980s – including Scottish plays – were united in their anti-Thatcherism. "So despite diversity – Howard Brenton, Caryl Churchill, David Hare and April de Angelis are all quite different writers – they were unified by being against the Tories. When Thatcher quit government, there was a void, and that was filled by a new generation of playwrights which included Sarah Kane and Mark Ravenhill, and Scottish writers such as David Greig and David Harrower. These writers, especially in London, had a fairly nihilistic view." In this narrative, the playwrights of the past 10 years have sometimes used popular forms or radical content, but have rarely united the two.

Generally, examples of the use of the past as an inspiration are readily available. John Tiffany, for example, remembers his university lecturer telling the class about John McGrath, and defines radical populism as "a populist movement against the prevailing elitism of the times". And Jack Bradley mentions not only McGrath's 7.84 theatre company, but also plays by Steve Gooch and Paul Thompson:

> "At one point, Steve and Paul did a play about Henry Ford [*The Motor Show*, 1974] and took it to the Ford factory at Dagenham. The idea of radical populism makes me think of 1970s shows by companies which had the words 'stock' or 'red' in their names. There are precious few companies now which have a political remit enshrined in their *raison d'être*.

The 7.84 Scotland theatre company is one of the rare survivors of that era."

Over the past 20 years, one of the irreversible effects of Thatcherism in the arts has been a narrowing of horizons. Jeanie O'Hare says that radical populism is "not a term I use in my working day", and Nicola Wilson sums up the attitude of many by saying, "No mainstream theatre today would have an artistic policy that they would define as radical in the political sense." But, of course, she'd like "to put on plays that challenge the audience while entertaining them." Nina Steiger brings a transatlantic perspective on a discussion that might otherwise seem insular. Having previously worked in New York, she finds the concept of radical populism unfamiliar, and asks, "What is radical content nowadays? I really think that we need to demystify this concept." For her, Theatre de Complicite's *Mnemonic* (2002) would be a good example of familiar ideas being explored in a fresh and radical way. In general, if radical populism is a term which is marked by its leftwing past, and is widely perceived as out-dated, the questions it raises, for example about form and content, are still urgent and relevant.

The present: "reach a popular audience but not be anodyne"

Talking about radical populism in the context of today's theatre suggests that what is happening is that this concept in the process of being redefined. Paul Sirett, for instance, argues that "radical populism does exist today, but in a very diluted way. It's not as overt as it once was." As an example, he quotes the work of Sarah Kane, which is radical in form but is "never going to appeal to a mass audience because of its difficult nature". For Jeanie O'Hare, "radical populism means something that can reach a popular audience but not be anodyne." To be radically popular, it seems, you really have to go some way beyond popular culture. Sirett also points out that "there seems to have been divergence nowadays between serious political work, which is just serious political work, and entertainment, which is just entertainment".

In terms of political theatre, 2002 was a turning point. After a couple of years during which the energy seemed to have drained out of new writing, the Edinburgh Festival Fringe in 2002 and 2003 connected again with global politics. The *Guardian*'s arts correspondent noted: "After years in which even the hint of politics was a sure way of emptying theatres, there is a new hunger for plays questioning Britain's readiness to embark on foreign adventures." Examples given were two Scottish plays: Gregory Burke's *The Straits* and Henry Adam's *The People Next Door*, both staged at the Traverse in 2003. Similarly, the *Independent* newspaper reported that "2002 was the year when political theatre staggered from the shallow grave in which it was dumped some time in the early 1980s; 2003 is the year when the body began to dance." (5)

Roxana Silbert, who directed *The People Next Door*, says, "It's a farce, informed by the Dario Fo tradition. So it's populist in form." Noting the play's references to popular culture – *Trisha* and *Jerry Springer, The Simpsons* and gangsta rap – she also points out that "it's one of the first Scottish plays that tackles cultural diversity. It differs from Fo's work in being much less didactic. It's much more ambivalent. Its politics are personal." Jeanie O'Hare agrees: "In *The People Next Door* there's a real political understanding underneath the play, and Adam has chosen a very popular form and done it with great skill and affection." Silbert also points out that Douglas Maxwell's *Helmet* (Traverse, 2002) took a computer game form rather than a televisual form, and developed a narrative around that. She thinks that some Scottish writers "are going back to the well-made play. And using the well-made comedy to question the future: what do we want Scotland to be?" This introduces the powerful idea of a regional dimension to radical populism. Playwright Liz Lochhead suggests that, in Scotland, "There is a popular audience still here. In London, theatre is something that arty people do in particular places. Here, there's a genuine popular culture." (6)

Despite the success of young Scottish playwrights, the issue of cultural tourism still rears its head. As John Tiffany says,

> "It's an interesting historical moment. *The Straits* has gone down a storm in Edinburgh, but a friend of mine – whose views I respect – said something that puzzled me: she's feeling exhausted by seeing portrayals of lowlifes on stage for a middle-class audience. Now, obviously Greg's characters are working class: that's who he is, and what he knows. But it was very interesting that she not only sees audiences as middle class (which they are) but also she sees people like me and Greg as middle class (which we're not) dabbling with so-called lowlifes. Middle-to-upper class theatre practitioners constantly put working-class characters on stage, but when you are working class (like me and Greg) then what are you meant to do?"

Tiffany indicates that one of the radical aspects of Burke's play is that the Paines Plough production used Frantic Assembly's Steven Hoggett, whose movement work with the cast gave the play a dreamlike feel. "Frantic's sources are very populist – film, music video and contemporary dance – and the audiences, especially young audiences, warm to that." He compares this with McGrath's use of the vaudeville form: "The radical thing is not that it is avant-garde but that it's a reaction to the elite of the day. Literary theatre seems safe while radical populism can scare critics because they don't grasp all its references." His manifesto is a provocative approach to form: "Naturalistic productions should be made illegal."

Even the National Theatre wants to experiment in form. The arrival of its new artistic director, Nicholas Hytner, in 2003 resulted in the production of his signature piece: *Jerry Springer: the Opera*. A mixture of television culture (the chat show) and high art (sophisticated music and operatic singing); the play was a box office hit and transferred to the West End in October 2003. Jeanie O'Hare says, "It marries a popular form with a high art form, and comes up with something very unexpected and very entertaining. It's radical in that it shifts people's perspective about what's possible in theatre." And, moreover, "It makes some sense of the effect that chat shows have on us, and suggests that the dramas of those who appear on them are on a grand scale." Jack Bradley, however, suggests that "the reason it has mass appeal is that it exploits a phenomenon which has a universal frame of reference. We've all seen Oprah or Trisha or Jerry, and so we immediately get the joke." The show's badge is its irony, but "it also makes the audience feel good because it is able to look down on the sados in it. As a result, it makes people feel smugly superior. It's populist rather than radical." Cultural tourism rides again. For Bradley, the National's most radical experiment has been to offer £10 seats for many of its large-stage shows. A huge box office success, this has broadened the audience. Typically, the scheme allows a couple to bring their children with them, perhaps for the first time. "So, for a new generation, their first exposure to *Henry V* is Adrian Lester [a black actor] playing an English king in an up-to-the-minute look at patriotism in the context of the Iraq War. This is a classic text done in a radical populist way, using multimedia: video, film, etc."

Yet much new writing remains traditional in terms of form. Bradley uses Kwame Kwei-Armah's *Elmina's Kitchen* (National, 2003; West End, 2005), a play about black youth and gun crime, to make a distinction: "Formally, Kwame's models are the well-made plays of August Wilson. His play has a socio-political intent rather than an ideological intent. It's not a critique of the political establishment but a critique of a prevailing social condition." He argues that the play "is both radical and populist. Radical in the way it exposes a massive social problem; populist in its use of the form of West Indian popular theatre." By contrast, a play such as Peter Gill's *The York Realist* (Royal Court, 2002) would have been an example of radical populism 40 years ago because of its subject matter – a gay love affair in a provincial town – but now feels like nostalgia. Given that neither play seems particularly radical either in form or in content, Bradley's championing of *Elmina's Kitchen* seems like special pleading.

Nor is he the only one to do this. For Graham Whybrow, an example of radical populism would be

Michael Wynne's comedy *The People Are Friendly* (Royal Court, 2002), which staged a debate between a Birkenhead father who is a shipyard worker and his daughter, a consultant who is managing the yard's redevelopment. "His plays seem to be quite broad and popular and jovial, but he uses that to smuggle in some more challenging themes." Similarly, Nicola Wilson says that an example of the Bush Theatre's radical populism would be Richard Cameron's *The Glee Club* (2002). "On one level, this was a nostalgic musical; on the other, it packed a political message about homophobia in the 1960s." At the same venue, Helen Blakeman's *Caravan* started as soap opera and then became uncomfortable study of teenage damage. For Paul Sirett, Adrian Jackson's production of *Pericles* by Cardboard Citizens (2003), using homeless or recently homeless amateur actors along with RSC professionals, and weaving the true stories of asylum seekers into Shakespeare's play, is a good example of how a classic can be made more populist. None of these examples are particularly convincing, however. In each case, the argument can only be sustained by picking out aspects of a production. True radical populism would not need this kind of sleight of hand.

Lisa Goldman, artistic director of the Red Room, which has a good track record in developing innovative drama and political theatre, is critical of the clichés about radical populism. "My feeling about radical populism is that context is crucial. You can only really understand the work of Littlewood and

McGrath, for example, if you look at its social context. It doesn't make much sense to talk of radical populism in the abstract." For her, debased ideas of radical populism "imply that on some level you're playing to the lowest common denominator". One of the reasons that she stopped working at Stratford East (as an assistant director in the early 1990s) was her frustration "with the attitude that said the audience won't understand, so quite good pieces of work were turned into quite poor pieces of work". Two Red Room shows, Kay Adshead's *The Bogus Woman* (2000) and Anthony Neilson's *Stitching* (2002), "were radical in that they push at the edges of form and audience expectation, and both were quite provocative." At the moment, she argues that "the term public theatre is more useful than political theatre because it implies that access is one of the major problems in taking theatre forward as an art form and renewing its social relevance." Like many, she well understands the problem of coterie audiences in London.

Emma Schad, one of the founder members of Artists Against The War, is also critical of debased ideas of radical populism. "Is there a difference between radical populism and popular radicalism? Is the onus on something being radical but which got away with it because people enjoyed it so much, or is the onus is on something being popular but asking vital questions at the same time?" She points out that "it's easier to define how popular something is (bums on seats) than how radical it is." *The People Next Door* is populist "in the sense that it's a sitcom and is accessible, but it's not easy in its content". For her, *Gagarin Way* is "more a play about politics than a political play". If "you define political theatre as a form that can change people's hearts and minds then there are very few examples of this today."

Both Goldman and Schad are sceptical about the hype surrounding *Jerry Springer: The Opera,* refusing to see anything radical in its content. And, while acknowledging that plays by young Scottish writers are full of ideas, they point out that that doesn't make a work either political or radical. On the other hand, Kay Adshead's *The Bogus Woman,* is a one-woman show about asylum seekers written with a mix of realism and poetry, which avoids a feel good ending, and is a cry of protest against British asylum regulations. It feels very contemporary not only because of its subject matter but also because of its experiential form. Adshead's next play, *Animal* (Red Room, 2003), was a less successful account of a dystopia where riot police switch from cracking heads to using psychotropic drugs and gas. Both plays carried an exciting political charge, and made good use of metaphor, but neither could be called populist.

The writers: "smashing the false mirror of realism"

What do playwrights themselves think of the relationship between form and content? Some answers to this question can be extrapolated from a series of articles published by the *Guardian* in 2003. These offer a sample of views on political theatre by a handful of writers. An early salvo came from Gregory Burke. He wrote how, following the worldwide success of *Gagarin Way*, he had been invited to many overseas premiers. "Everywhere I go, people expect me to have something to say about theatre – and politics. People think you have the answers. And I have been disappointing people everywhere." He says he prefers telling jokes to discussions about globalisation. Still, however flip, his serious point about the play is that "what it is mostly about is a community" and that "it is amazing how many countries have communities that are similar to the one in *Gagarin Way*." Political theatre, he believes, is not just about politics. (7)

Michael Wynne would probably agree. He says that in *The People Are Friendly*, both father and daughter are on the "same side politically" and their family conflict "reflects how muddled the lines have become". Wynne reports that at a Royal Court workshop on political theatre, the participants were asked to write down "what elements we thought were essential to a political play". One of these was to "change the audience's mind", and this "raised a few nervous laughs". How naive, how uncool, how 1970s – but the comment stayed in Wynne's mind. He argues that "most great political plays aren't about politics", and that laughter is as important as ideas, but he also ends up by hoping that "more writers will come out of the cupboard and say they are trying to write a big, ambitious, political play."

Although Burke and Wynne have mixed feelings about overtly political writing, Kentucky-born Naomi Wallace has no problem "with calling myself a political writer". But she does think that the word "political" might have an image problem: "most often it is used to mean theatre with a left-wing axe to grind." Instead, she suggests using the term "engaged". "Engaged, for example, with questions of power and its myriad forms – questions of who has it and who doesn't, and the reasons why." She admits to the unfashionable practice of writing "from ideas": "I write to explore theories." She certainly is not afraid of writing about either the personal or the political.

From a feminist perspective, veteran playwright Pam Gems argues, somewhat reductively, that "the irony is, all theatre is political in a profound way. Why? Because it is subversive." It can "change opinion, laugh prejudice out the door, soften hearts, awaken perception". But she suggests that overtly political plays are "awful" and "jejune" because they take themselves too seriously and are often written by people who have no experience of what they write. Her conclusion is that this is an example of cultural tourism. "There is something improper about the well-healed seeking to represent the disadvantaged."

Another older playwright, David Hare, says that "like many people of my background, I had chosen drama in the hope of using it to advance political ends", and suggests that one of the problems is that theatre itself "has changed as little as society". He ends up by passionately arguing that the most important question you can ask about a play is "What is it saying?" David Edgar, one of the market leaders of 1970s state-of-the-nation plays, sees obituaries of political theatre as premature. "I suspect that British political theatre will continue to be rehabilitated by new and established playwrights who understand there is no contradiction between writing about politics and writing about people."

Clearly, what needs to be criticised is the great tradition of British naturalistic social realism. For example, London-based Biyi Bandele argues that the play that first inspired him – *Look Back in Anger*, which he saw on television while growing up in Nigeria – derived its power "not from the literal-realism of its narrative but from the sheer verve of Osborne's pathology of the human, his bloody-minded reverse-humanism. The veracity of the world he has created is poetic, not literal; he deals not in road signs but in symbols." Similarly, David Greig, who has translated Albert Camus's *Caligula*, argues that the English tradition of "shorthand naturalism", where "the real world is brought into the theatre and plonked on the stage like a familiar old sofa", is limiting to the theatrical imagination. New writers should connect with a different tradition, that of Jean Anouilh, Samuel Beckett and Eugene Ionesco, "which smashes the false mirror of realism, forcing us to piece together a reflection of ourselves from glimpses in shards and fragments."

In his contribution, Kwame Kwei-Armah began by acknowledging that "so few" people "want to talk about politics these days". Then, after making several powerful points about being co-opted into a discussion that seemed to ignore the question of race, he described the work of the Blue Mountain theatre company, which specialises in "a brand of bawdy Jamaican comedy" playing to "sellout audiences in huge auditoriums". Black artists, he concluded, should respond to the challenge of such companies by trying to tap into "that audience and introduce it to challenging narratives". In common with most of the contributors, Kwei-Armah's aspirations are clearer than his practice. One of the problems with *Elmina's Kitchen* is that although it was a cry from the heart, there was nothing in its content that suggested any possibility of a solution. Playwrights are better at identifying what's wrong than at saying what to do about it. At worst, this can feel like an abnegation of responsibility.

The future: "theatre needs a bomb under it"

Once again, political theatre is firmly on the cultural agenda. There are newspaper and magazine articles, public platforms, radio conversations, web chats and even the occasional mention on television. (8) But the dominant form, the verbatim dramas – exemplified by the Tricycle Theatre's tribunal plays or David Hare's Stuff Happens (National, 2004) – feel neither radical, nor particularly populist. They tell us what we already know, and what we can find out about outside the theatre. Of much more resonance, are plays such as Martin Crimp's *Cruel and Tender* (Young Vic, 2004) which use metaphor and imagination rather than the literal reproduction of reality. But what about the future?

When theatre-makers are asked to speculate, they mix caution with flashes of optimism. For example, Lisa Goldman says,

> "Because there's been such resistance to the War on Terror, and there is a renewed questioning going on in society, it might be that we're due for a new wave of theatre which reflects that movement. At the moment, theatre needs a bomb under it. The whole system is still geared to the Oxbridge elite, a very narrow stratum of society. In some ways, things are worse than they were 30 years ago."

Nicola Wilson adds, "When political plays arrive [at the Bush], they are already out of date. We got a lot of 9/11 plays, but by the time we'd read them something else had happened." She rightly suggests that "young writers need to use allegory and metaphor much more. When we ask young writers to write political plays they tend to write about politicians rather than about politics. They are a bit afraid of the subject matter." Roxana Silbert puts the problem clearly: "Having politics in it doesn't make a play good or bad. That said, a good political play should show the possibility of what might be, rather than just what is." For her, a play such as *Trainspotting* is a very strong representation of the world as it is, "but there's a danger that if you simply show things as they are, you're not bringing a more imaginative perspective to it. You don't see where they are coming from and what they might be in the future." The political theatre of the future needs urgently to expand the imaginative horizons of its audiences, and to contest the closing down of the imagination by commercial mass media.

Graham Whybrow confirms that the current trend is to move away from the in-yer-face directness of the 1990s. "A group of writers are now maturing into probing the whole question of the present and the past, and responsibility, so that plays are becoming more diagnostic and less symptomatic." The present can only be understood by looking at the past. So Richard Bean in *Under the Whaleback* (Royal Court, 2003) chose not to write a continuous action workplay, but a series of three snapshots showing how a community evolved through recent history. Roy Williams in *Fallout* (Royal Court, 2003) chose not to show the brutal murder at the heart of his story but the consequences of the killing. Although neither can be described as a young writer, both examine personal choice and responsibility.

Looking to the future, Jeanie O'Hare says, "We've got to get out of the cul-de-sac of authenticity. There are three ingredients in a good writer: instinctive rawness, linguistic invention and concern with ideas. If you have all three of those, you have something very exciting." Young writers often have the rawness and linguistic invention but not the ideas. "They need to learn from the physical theatre companies and to trust metaphor a bit more." Nina Steiger says that, despite the commercial imperative in British theatre, "Trying to anticipate market tastes is futile – it's like chasing your own tail." Jack Bradley concludes, "Nature abhors a vacuum, and there is room for more radical populism because when you give audiences something of substance, they are willing to grapple with it, and will come." He points out that "it's only called populist if it's successfully popular. If you have to stress one of the two words, 'radical populism', it's the populist you should pursue." Bearing in mind Wilkie Collins's secret of writing – "Make 'em laugh, make 'em cry, make 'em wait!" – Bradley's slogan is: "Make 'em laugh, make 'em cry, make 'em think!"

So wither radical populism? The widespread perception that it belongs to a bygone age suggests that the bumpy terrain between radical populism and cultural tourism has been subsumed into questions of form and content, and access, rather than resolved. Still, it is clear that in an atmosphere in which political theatre is enjoying a flourishing revival, urgent questions about style remain. The dominance of naturalistic social realism, on one hand, and verbatim drama, on the other, has marginalised those plays which have a more imaginative, and experimental, aesthetic style. These may be radical in content, or radical in form, or both, but they seemed to be doomed to play to metropolitan coterie audiences in small studio theatres. My guess is that reinvigorating old theatrical forms will prove less exciting theatrically than the development of new ones. But, then, British theatre does have a knack of springing surprises.

Notes

1) Burke notes: "The play is named after a street in the village of Lumphinnans in West Fife which was a hotbed of communism" and is an account of what happened "to leftwing politics in the wake of globalisation" (*Gagarin Way*, London: Faber, 2001, p iv).

2) John McGrath, *A Good Night Out: Popular Theatre – Audience, Class and Form*, London: Nick Hern, 2nd ed, 1996, p 11.

3) Red Room, 'Going Public: First Questions/Provocations', leaflet, February 2003.

4) All quotations from the following interviews: Paul Sirett, writer and former literary manager of the Royal Shakespeare Company: 29 July 2003; Roxana Silbert, artistic director of Paines Plough new writing company, formerly literary manager of the Traverse Theatre, Edinburgh: 5 August 2003; Graham Whybrow, literary manager of the Royal Court: 6 August 2003; John Tiffany, literary manager of the National Theatre of Scotland, formerly of Paines Plough: 12 August 2003; Jack Bradley, literary manager of the National Theatre: 29 August 2003; Lisa Goldman, artistic director of the Red Room: 7 September 2003; Emma Schad, founder member of Artists Against The War: 18 September 2003; Jeanie O'Hare, literary manager of the RSC, formerly of the Hampstead Theatre: 26 September 2003; Nicola

Wilson, former literary manager of the Bush Theatre: 1 October 2003; Nina Steiger, literary manager of the Soho Theatre: 2 October 2003.

5) Fiachra Gibbons, 'Fringe Favourites Take Aim at Politics', *Guardian*, 7 August 2003, and Johann Hari, 'The Left Isn't Always Right', *Independent*, 21 August 2003.

6) Quoted in Brian Logan, 'Northern Exposure', *Guardian*, 7 August 2003.

7) All articles from the *Guardian*: Gregory Burke, 'Funny Peculiar', 12 April 2003; Michael Wynne, 'Humour Me', 3 May 2003; Naomi Wallace, 'Strange Times', 29 March 2003; Pam Gems, 'Not in Their Name', 17 May 2003; David Hare, 'All Back to the Canteen', 24 May 2003; David Edgar, 'Secret Lives', 19 April 2003; Biyi Bandele, 'Read Between the Signs', 26 April 2003; David Greig, 'A Tyrant for All Time', 28 April 2003; Kwame Kwei-Armah, 'Primary Colours', 10 May 2003.

8) For example, Lisa Goldman and Joyce McMillan, 'Staging our protests', *Guardian*, 2 August 2003; 'Political Theatre Special', *Front Row*, BBC Radio 4, 21 April 2003; and 'Debate: Political Theatre', *TheatreVoice* website, http://www.theatrevoice.com/the_archive/, 26 September 2003.

<u>Absolute immediacy</u>

Scott Graham

In conversation with Nina Steiger

[Scott Graham is co-founder, along with Vicki Middleton and Steven Hoggett, of the UK theatre company Frantic Assembly. Established in 1994, the company has distinguished itself for its highly physical performance vocabulary, and its innovative staging of both devised, and writer-based work. Influenced by films, bands, video, club dancing, and other aspects of pop culture, they have been able to create consistently innovative, progressive work for the theatre over the years. Their ability to create pieces that reach an audience with rare immediacy has been their hallmark almost since their inception. In shows like their landmark piece <u>Hymns</u> (1999), written by Chris O'Connell, they created a devastatingly visceral work about emotional dysfunction amongst young men, and death. With its jump-cut moves culled from contemporary dance and film, and its hurtling story-telling style, the piece set the stage for the kind of eloquent, daring, and funny work Frantic Assembly would make over time. In subsequent pieces, they have explored multifaceted collaborations with the

UK band Lamb (Peepshow, 2002), and Manchester, UK's live art venue for young people Contact (Tiny Dynamite, 2001). In February 2004 they joined forces with equally progressive UK companies Paines Plough, and Graeae to stage Glyn Cannon's On Blindness at Soho Theatre in London. On Blindness is a play about blind people who can see things as they are, and sighted people who cannot. The cast was a mixture of disabled and non-disabled performers. In May of 2005 they created the site-specific piece Dirty Wonderland, with text by Michael Wynne, for the Brighton Festival. The piece was staged in more than thirty rooms and spaces of the art deco Grand Ocean Hotel before its conversion into flats. Projects in development include collaboration with dramatist Mark Ravenhill, and a co-production of The Changeling with West Yorkshire Playhouse.

This interview was conducted in February 2004 by Nina Steiger, international literary associate of Soho Theatre (London) whilst Frantic Assembly was in rehearsal with On Blindness. As befits this volume, which seeks, in part, to erase the hierarchy of 'high' language over 'low' language, and as befits Frantic Assembly's democratic approach to pop culture, there has been an effort to preserve the informal, off-the-cuff manner of the original conversation, and moreover, of Graham's responses. – Caridad Svich]

NS: How has the company grown over the last five years and how have the shows, goals and esthetics changed with that growth?
SG: I think the company was always about energy and about enthusiasm and that's what got us through the first few years because it was financial very, very difficult and the people we were at the time and the people that surrounded us – we all shared that. But it was always our goal to get somewhere where we could pay someone honestly for his or her work.

And after a few years we were lucky enough to get to that status - and that's improved over recent years as well and that has transformed the company massively. We now have the opportunity to do different scale works and shows, and to work with different people: with writers and existing plays. Before, a lot of the work happened within the rehearsal room, because we wanted to make contact with other practitioners. Right from the start the collaborative process was about what could be learned from other people and again, this was about extending out, outside ourselves.

NS: DO you think actors are often wary of "the devising process" as a method or are it really just a difference of approach?
SG: I think both. With genuine good reason. The devising process – there isn't THE devising process. Most people have had a bad experience with one and if they think that's the only one, then that colors their approach to being involved in such a process. I'm fairly lucky in that most of our devising process has gone really well. But that's because of always being very tightly structured and always being inspired by the words. People think about improv as being freedom but you can only actually find the freedom in improv if you set yourself some very strict parameters, otherwise you just spin off and you find you rely on what you know and that's not freedom, that's actually trapping yourself.

We never improv now any longer than three or four minutes. We put a track of music on and when that finishes we stop. And I know some people find a lot of good stuff by improving for two hours. We will probably improv for two hours but we do it in five-minute sections instead.
NS: What are some of the other techniques you have used?
SG: The first thing we will do is get to know the script really well. So we will attack that script in the first week in exactly the same way

a company like a text-based company like Paines Plough would. From then, we've found that we set up a game or exercise with performers, extremely simple, [one that] may even involve patterns on the stage and you just gradually get them to become aware of the possibilities of interaction on the stage and with all that they know from the play, that starts to, all these possibilities that pop up in meetings and occurrences and touches… The space really starts to fizz with possibility. It's not about saying "right we're going to do an exercise now that's going to be the end scene and you're going to throw this person around here" because our performers come from so many different backgrounds, we need to find some common ground and that is in the possibilities of what we can all do and so we need to get people tuned into that as quickly as possible.

Actors aren't always required or invited to be part of the audience in the process. We do invite our actors to step out and see what other people are doing, keep in touch what other people are doing because we often split rehearsals as well so that people work in different corners of the room. Some actors might find that difficult – because it's about their process as well and what's going on inside. And I respect that completely. And that really does work for them on other shows. But we've had to define our process and it's probably about being slightly less selfish for the actor (and I don't mean selfish in a derogatory way – I mean it in a descriptive way). We do like performers to have a really good idea of what the overall theatrical intention is and not to lose their character in that at all but in the early days to have an idea of why there are other people in this room as well, why there are lighting designers sitting in the room and why lighting designers are willing to comment on the choreography. Because we will ask that as well. Whereas I think an actor needs to be aware that that's a possibility and to be invited in to that, that's a positive thing because they are going to be the inspiration for the lighting as much as the words are. So it can sound like a massive committee – and it can sound like it can go absolutely nowhere. So without enforcing it too strongly I think it's a kind of natural understanding and we can manage people quite well in that environment.

NS: Soho Theatre Company is writer-based and this project *On Blindness* is uniquely so as well. What attracts you to a script and where does the writer fit into the process behind this project?

SG: I love the imagination of the writer, I love their skill – I admire and I envy it. I love the worlds they create and I love to try and 1) do justice to that and 2) get inside their world. The third thing is that that's just words on a page and the imagination of a writer and the imagination of a reader. Those things aren't necessarily the same thing – the 2 imaginations. The writer can guide and I think there's a lot that can found. I don't believe theatre exists in a rehearsal room and I don't think theatre exists within the bindings of a play either. Theatre exists between performers, lighting, the audience, the music and that moment on that day because shows are very different from day to day. Audiences are very different; their experience is very different too. And that, I think, is theatre and it defines *itself* actually.

The building is called the theatre and we sometimes forget that. We spend an awful lot of time in a rehearsal room, spouting self-justification and talking about ourselves. But I think there's lots of room in writing and lots of things that a writer can learn from performers and from ourselves, we've got a much more physical way of seeing things. And for Glyn Cannon with *On Blindness*, or for any writer, I would say there are some things that you don't have to say; there are other ways of saying them, which are much more economical. It always seems to be what we're aiming for – maximum economy. And the thing that's great about good writers is that they recognise that as well and embrace that. So that's where the two worlds meet. If a writer's trying to create a world on a page, they've got to realise that when it becomes physical and 3-dimensional, there are other ways and there are other possibilities and we give writers ways to embrace that.

NS: How has the three-way co-production between Frantic Assembly, Graeae and Paines Plough worked?

SG: Frantic Assembly and Paines Plough have a history from *Tiny Dynamite* and we found a way of working there. Plus the designer Julian Crouch and composer Nick Powell on this project worked on *Tiny Dynamite.* So we all found a way of working together and absolutely loved working on that show. So it is different with Graeae but the most immediate thing Graeae offers is an ability to communicate to an audience that we have, not consciously but just through ignorance, neglected. We thought we can say what the writer wants to say through our physicality and the writer doesn't need to speak. Well here's another company that says 'no that's not good enough sometimes and you need to do this.'

And also what Paines Plough offers in Artistic Director Vicky Featherstone is an amazing understanding of text and the possibilities and the relationship between words and the actors is just continually opening up the text and the theatrical possibilities. So there are three very clear areas of expertise. But we've also got a kind of working practice, which blends all of that completely, and it's something that we feel very comfortable in. And yet it's also incredibly refreshing to learn new things every day. Sometimes you learn new things by clashing. 50 % of this particular rehearsal process is also about sitting where you're very, very comfortable as well and that might not be the case in every co-production. I would guess it isn't.

We didn't enter into lightly at all. We entered into it because we – I'm going back to *Tiny Dynamite*. It was about Vicky Featherstone, myself and Steven Hoggett wanting to work together because we felt it would work personally and we found out there were things we did that just fitted in brilliantly for us. And then Abi Morgan was brought in to write the text.

NS: The workshop process is one we rely on heavily at Soho. It's something done by a lot of companies and it means different things to everyone. When you're workshopping, before going into production, what is involved that process for you?

SG: We've trained ourselves in a slightly different way. We see theatre, our work anyway, as entertainment and it's got to be ready as an entertainment on the first day. We also see that that will develop massively as a given. But the impetus is to create a cracking piece of entertainment that people are going to say 'YES.' If we go back from there, then there is a defined rehearsal period of 6 weeks that will have a fairly natural structure to it for us. Before then, we will have discussions and many meetings with the writer and there might be scripts going back and forth and developing but there's very little workshopping.

Steven Hoggett and I have a lot more flexibility and a lot of the ideas for the show; the impetus for the show often comes from us, as we're co-artistic directors of Frantic Assembly. We want to make a show about this; we talk to a writer about this particular idea, develop that, and push on. But the rehearsal process often starts on day one with the script and finishes on the day of the show. And there's very rarely a time when we ran a workshop to see what was there.

NS: As Frantic Assembly has committed to creating pieces for entertainment, they are relying on and offering an alternative to the mainstream pop culture. How do you use pop culture itself to do this?

SG: Pop culture is our starting point. Films, adverts, music videos, music itself. Those are very much our reference points. We want to achieve something onstage that's as good as or has the qualities of, has the effect of things we've seen. If we take that as our starting point or something we want to aim towards then we will use anything to get there. In *Peepshow,* a collaboration with the band Lamb and playwright Isabel Wright (2002), one of our inspirations was an advert for Levi's jeans where a couple ran through walls and kept going. In theatre you can't do that, you can't burst through walls. Well, you can, but your walls will be shit and everyone will know.

So we wanted to create that feeling, wanted that to be a reference point. So we unashamedly took that and ran with it and used whatever we could. So it was this dance. We lulled the audience into the rules of dance before they started exploding through walls. And the audience was ready to believe that they exploded through walls completely.

Elsewhere we talk about music, films, and adverts. All the time. Absolutely all the time and those are our reference points, our benchmarks, and that filters through to the show and I suppose it's that sensibility of our own which actually quite pulpy. Pop-y and that's what comes through and what might make the work pop-y or popular.

What Steven and myself have always said is that we reserve the right to make shows about ourselves and shows that we like. For years we've called a theatre for young people. And what people fail to realise is that we've been making shows for ourselves all that time and it's a coincidence. We've actively marketed towards young people and we've been very successful but the shows have been what we've wanted to make. And one of the reasons we've reserved the right to make shows about ourselves is that we're trying to warn people that we're getting older and our audiences aren't. Well, they kind of are but every time a school comes, next year when that school comes, I'm a year older and they're not. So that gap grows every year and if we're going to make shows about ourselves, there's going to be a time possibly when we don't quite speak the same language [as our audience.] I think we are inspired by what's around us, and it's not about seeing other theatre. It's something far more immediate.

I think people underestimate the creativity and expertise existing in the fields of videos and advertising. There are a lot of shit adverts, a lot of shit videos. But the good ones are almost completely groundbreaking because they have to be and those people go on to do bigger and better things. So if you want to see where the best filmmakers of the next five years, well they're making adverts and videos now.

And that gives us a massive, massive thrill. There's something about theatre that is about catching up. Director Vicky Featherstone has been making fantastic work for years. And she still appears in the stage as she did last year as One To Watch. New Kids On The Block in theatre are basically anybody under 40. And to me that's fairly ridiculous. Because they didn't start when they were 35 – they have actually been doing it and doing great work. It's that the balance in theatre is so top-heavy. It's only validated at such a level and is dismissed. It's so London-centric and so geared towards the word. Play and theatre as being a text. What Soho offers is the development, where the development with the writer and theatre is very, very immediate and part of that process ends up in a text being bound. But, where theatre comes about taking scripts off of the shelf and doing it, that can be wonderful but it can also be a bit of a move towards a video culture, you know, where you take something off a shelf and either do it, watch an old film because you enjoy it or do it to slightly reinvent it. There's nothing necessarily wrong with that but there's a whole kind of vibrancy that's not taken seriously within theatre.

What theatre also has more than probably any other art form is a massive amount of shit because people want to do it and aren't necessarily good enough to do it. And at that lower level, it's hard to see good stuff. And I suppose that's where the conservativeness of theatre is, because it's so easy to waste a large part of your life trying to find good stuff and people would rather pay a little bit more and go to the National because it's got some kind of quality – even if that's turgid and dull. At least it was Judi Dench being turgid and dull.

NS: How do ancient ideas of ritual, myth or legend weave into the work? And with dance and movement and even the act of making theatre as ancient form, how do you start to blend these oldest ideas of expression with the news ones in pop culture?

SG: I think a lot of this is to do with the fact that we don't come from an academic theatrical background. We're not trained as performers or anything like that. Obviously we're English graduates. We got switched onto theatre on one particular day that I remember. There was a moment for me where I suddenly became really awakened to theatre and its possibilities and from that moment onwards something in me had changed and I decided I wanted to try something out. And exactly the same thing happened to Steven at exactly the same moment.

NS: What was it?!

SG: I went to see a show that he was in and it was the Drama Society at Swansea University being directed by Volcano Theatre Company and it was a quite stunning show – *Savages* by Christopher Hampton. So from then on, theatre has always been incredibly immediate – everything I've learnt has been in that moment and I've never picked up a book and learned anything about theatre or sat in a lecture and been told about any of the rituals. SO it's only ever meant anything to me in the moment.

In terms of rituals and myths, we all carry their significance, we're all touched by it, but I can actually only really assess them in the moment and I'm sure that's the same for Steven as well. So it's entirely natural for us to talk about something that may seem ancient *along with* pop videos, because what we're actually talking about with pop videos is the effect of them. What they made us feel, how somebody achieved something. The technical stuff is of massive interest to us but it's not really what we're talking about because we witnessed it, it had an effect on us and what we're talking about then is something that is ancient as well. It's a human response. And a very immediate response. It's the reason why we phone each other late at night, because we've seen something on the telly or an advert has come on and 'you must see this!'

CABARET AS DRAMA

(with apologies to Joseph Kerman)

Michael Friedman

Imagine…
First, the announcement of the event: A concert in the palace of the now-deposed emperor and his wife, open to the public, "whereby these rooms might at last be rendered useful to the people" The placards continue:

> People! The gold that glitters on these walls is the product of your toil! For long enough your work has nourished and your blood has quenched the thirst of the insatiable monster…Revolution has made you free; at last you may claim your rightful property. This land is yours.[1]

Shopkeepers, little old ladies, soldiers, housewives, workers, well-dressed ladies fill the rooms—the gilt railing and stairs hung

---

[1] Edwards, Stewart. *The Communards of Paris*. Cornell University Press, Ithaca, 1973. p. 148.

with bedding and stocking. People scratch their names on the walls with pencil, ink, and knives. The imperial banners and emblems hang beside defaced portraits of generals and princes. It is 8 o'clock, and the rooms are full, and still over 2,000 people remain, waiting for admittance.

Now a woman has taken the stage. She wears a black gown, bare décolletage, a scarlet sash, and stands in a stark, defiant pose. She sings to the crowd one of her songs of the café-concert:

> In the heart of Paris's mire
> There lives a race of iron born.
> Deep in its soul a raging fire
> That burns the flesh from body torn.
> All of its children born in slums
> And if you see them I think you'll know why:
> They are the lowest scum!
> But so am I!

The crowd is in frenzy. They clap; they stamp their feet. The singer reprises the refrain. Outside in the palace gardens, thousands listen to the applause from inside, while in the distance the sounds of distant bombing compete with the display. The lights of the bombs flash over the city like fireworks. The next day the massacre of the citizenry by the distant army begins.[2]

Or imagine:
The woman is on trial for "unlawfully preparing, advertising, giving, directing, presenting and participating in an obscene, indecent, immoral, and impure drama, play, exhibition, show and entertainment, and obscene, indecent, immoral and impure scenes, tableaux, incidents…"[3] She was arrested on the night of the second performance of this show, along with her entire company of 54 performers, who play drag queens, gay acrobats, chorus girls and boys, married song and dance teams, stage hands, producers, and other vaudevillians. The show was packed, the audience eager to see if the police would raid. When they did, a drag queen began to rant against police oppression. The woman is arrested to wild, supportive applause. In its arguments, the Prosecution notes that the show has been designed "to appeal to the sort of people that might be attracted to the theatre by a show of this character."[4] $60,000 dollars poorer, she is acquitted of all charges. Within a few years, she will be the country's most notorious movie star.[5]

---

[2] Ibid. pp.144-148.
[3] Schlissel, Lillian. *Three Plays by Mae West*. Lillian Schlissel, ed. Routledge, New York, 1977. p. 222.
[4] Ibid.
[5] Schlissel, Lillian. "Introduction." *Three Plays by Mae*

The first of these scenes is the great performance of La Bordas, one of the originators of modern cabaret performance, in May 1871 at the Tuileries Palace, in a concert given by the Commune of Paris, which had seized control of Paris and lasted just over two months. Just after the concert the French government, which had fled to Versailles, sent in the army and killed over 25,000 Parisians, many of whom had attended the concert.

The second is trial of Mae West in 1928 for her play *The Pleasure Man* after its premiere at the Biltmore Theatre in New York. The play, which centered on vaudevillian performers, including transvestites and homosexuals, ends in the castration of its title character, a Don Juan. But it is most memorable as a tribute to performance, to the drag queens, dancing girls, acrobats, crooners, novelty acts who created the first original, and truly populist, entertainment in Vaudeville.

When I discuss "Cabaret" I am not referring to it as a place—an exclusive meeting place of artists, a nightclub, a smoky room--but as a style, a way of performing, not merely part of a specific tradition within a historical period (the "cabaret era" of fin-de-siècle Europe, the "cabaret" culture of mid-century New York),

---

West. Lillian Schlissel, ed. Routledge, New York, 1977. pp. 18-28.

but drawing on a long tradition. Cabaret in this sense is the idea of a certain kind of performance and its relationship to the audience--half play, half concert, certainly personality-based, not a replacement for theatre, but an alternative, the way vaudeville provided an alternative for legitimate theatre and commedia for the court theatre. Cabaret is, above all, illegitimate. In fact, I am not sure that there is a better description for it than the one given by the District Attorneys of New York: an obscene, indecent, immoral, and impure drama, play exhibition, show and entertainment.

To be honest about it, Cabaret has never been a populist genre. Its origins as a late nineteenth-century proto-modernist movement are in the salon, not in the popular theatre. By definition it was a hermetic movement, a place for artists to create art away from conservative culture and politics. Based in the idea of *kleinkunst*, "small art" or "art in small forms," Cabaret was opposed to the monumental forms of late-19th century high art and kitsch. For the artists of the cabaret, these small forms included popular song, pantomime, puppet, shadow play, circus, variety show, poetry, parody, street-song, dance, short plays and sketches, and monologues. Here was a way to merge the worlds of high and low art, without losing the piquancy of either. Harold Segel writes, "If Cabarets were from the outset elitist virtually by definition, the art for which they became best known was anything but that. It aimed, above all, at ending the hegemony of art that was either elitist by virtue of patronage or audience, or bourgeois by virtue of its standards and conventions."[6] Street-songs were shocking in their simplicity and in the sordidness of their subjects. Parody allowed for the mockery of the current artistic and social climate. As part of the "crisis" which led to modernism, cabaret was paradoxically a form of political and social discourse, and a hotbed of the idea of art's existence for its own sake, its essential purposelessness.

In America, despite such valiant efforts as John Wanamaker's genre-crossing "Upstairs at the Downstairs," Lenny Bruce, Mabel Mercer, Carol Burnett singing "I Made a Fool of Myself Over John Foster Dulles," Ben Bagley's "forbidden" reviews, Lily Tomlin, Mort Stahl, Woody Allen, and of course The Revuers' merry antics crossing over into legitimate work with the likes of Leonard Bernstein, cabaret has remained something apart, alone—a kind of specialised entertainment, and possibly an acquired taste.

---

[6] Segel, Harold B. *Turn-of-the-century cabaret : Paris, Barcelona, Berlin, Munich, Vienna, Cracow, Moscow, St. Petersburg, Zurich.* Columbia University Press, New York, 1987. p. xvii.

Romantic as I find the possibility of small rooms with performances for artists by artists, I think the idea of performance without an audience is, essentially, a dead end. In current theatre, how many performances do we see that are competent, even excellent, but that strike us with their lack of a point, with the uncertainty that they had any reason to exist at all. For whom exactly are these plays being performed? (This is a problem plaguing commercial theatre designed for group sales as much as experimental theatre designed for a few stout individuals.) This kind of deadly performance has become the norm. Art should have a purpose, should matter, which is not to say that art needs to be dealing with issues, that its content need be *important*. Too many shows seem to take their "important" content as a sign that the performance itself is at all vital for the audience.

Granted, this list of American performers I described above includes a wide variety of performers; Bruce and Burnett, while both "comics," approach the form from drastically different stylistic points. But what is important about all of the performances mentioned above is that they are, specifically, "performances." The genre being explored is not exactly acting, not exactly singing, but something that is virtuosic, "show-offy," and that is, most importantly, connected to the audience. If some of these performers come close to stand-up comedy, some to musical theatre, and some to concert, if Lenny Bruce's politics are confrontational while Carol Burnett's are ironic (and almost romantic), that just shows how wide the possibilities are—what is true about both Burnett and Bruce, and the other performers mentioned, is that they are working without a safety net. This is the ideal of cabaret-theatre.

What do I mean by cabaret-theatre? I can probably best start with what I do not mean (this is a personal, arbitrary, and, I am sure, maddening list):

Concerts
Stand-up comedy or Improv
Theatre for Children
Performances of Classics
American Musical Theatre
Avant-garde Theatre

What is cabaret-theatre? It is:

Presentational
Musical
Sexy
Popular
Inexpensive
Dangerous
Messy
Connected

If the last of these sounds like E.M. Forster at his most optimistic, all the better. If any performance these days can only connect, it has already succeeded beyond all dreams.

Where is cabaret in American theatre? It survives, nominally, in nightclubs where singers, some brilliant, some terrible, sing standards with a two-drink minimum. It survives as a sort of collegiate black-box setting, as in the Yale Drama School's cabaret, where raucous productions of new and old plays are performed for drunken graduate students and others. It certainly survives in the rock concert. But since the death of vaudeville in the early part of the century, and the death of nightclubs as a way to stardom in the middle of the century (think of Doris Day, Nichols and May, Barbra Streisand, and many others), it is hard to see where theatre and a sort of off-the-cuff, musical, highly individual performance style meet much these days. Certainly in some performance art. Certainly in the work of the classical "downtown" theatre ensembles such as the Wooster Group. Certainly in the work of certain playwrights performed at certain theatres (I am thinking of Charles Mee and others) None of these examples strikes me as remarkably populist. But cabaret in America has, with the exception of its vaudeville roots, tended to be expensive, and therefore fancy.

The cabaret that gets reviewed as such in the New York Times, for example, is exclusively the kind typified by Hotel venues such as the Algonquin, the Carlyle, and others. It is not worth describing this kind of cabaret at its worst. At its best, as in the performances of Bobby Short, this can be a kind of transcendent excavation, a glamorous reconstruction of a style and a room and a way of living that are gone for good; a work of nostalgia. And the cornerstone of this rarified world is the standard. Some new songs and acts may be performed, but the centers of its repertoire are a group of songs by dead men. Bobby Short knew Cole Porter, and performs his work as a contemporary, but he is the last of a dying breed.

Where do La Bordas and her legacy fit into this? Her lineage, through the stars of the Belle Époque, through Edith Pilaf and Jacques Brel, Ethel Merman and Billie Holliday and Patti Smith and Nina Simone, and others, is partly that of particularly idiosyncratic singers performing tailor-made, *new* material. It has been hard to reconstruct in the twentieth century the kind of implied narrative between La Bordas and her audience—us against them, the sublimated cultural impulses of the lower classes, the "canaille," or scum of Paris—but in instances such as "Milord," "Mississippi Goddamn" and "Rock 'n Roll Nigger," there are some brave examples. These transcend whatever concert form they come out of to be some of the best examples of musical theatre, or cabaret theatre, of this century. It is the possibility of a point of view, of an individual voice and sound, of a political agenda, that separates La Bordas' progeny from the singers. Piaf, Brel, La Bordas, Smith, Holliday, Simone, even Merman—not one of them has a "pretty," maybe even a "beautiful," voice. They are dangerous—they might sound ugly, might be too loud, might go too far, and might just start screaming at you.

Perhaps what cabaret needs is censorship. The possibility of authoritarian disaster is certainly what lent urgency to the Berlin and Paris cabarets. Or perhaps we have evolved to a theatre of smoothness over a theatre of personality. The problem, as I see it, is that cabaret has devolved into *Cabaret*, a worthy musical by any means, but one in which the dangerous element that brought life to the Berlin forms that give the musical its setting, song-style (arguably), and cache has been replaced by a kind of relentless professionalism. (In a piece of spectacular irony, in fact, the Roundabout Theatre's recent production of *Cabaret* is in the process of closing, after a long run at Studio 54, the ghost of the great cabaret of the late '70s.) I, for one, admire this professionalism—it is the trait that makes the American musical such a worthy form—and, in any case, it is likely that *Cabaret* is a greater work than *The Pleasure Man*. But this very professionalism has removed from theatre, musical and otherwise, one of its central pleasures: the possibility of disaster. (Maybe the tenor will botch his note; maybe we'll go to jail; maybe tonight the show will end differently than it did yesterday). We don't tend to value messes these days (perhaps as the world gets messier, we prefer our entertainment tidy), but one has only to read the account of Busby Berkeley describing his forgotten lyrics to get a sense of what is lost in the tidiness.

It is the messiness that makes cabaret-theatre vital, which connects it to its roots in vaudeville, in Berlin, in the drag show, in the café-concert, in the opera house, in the music hall, on the showboat, in melodrama, in the commedia, the nightclub.

As *The Village Voice* and *The New York Times* continue to duke it out over whether directors like Robert Wilson have ruined American Theatre or whether they have saved it, they miss the more important question of why so much seems over-directed or under-directed these days, either airless or useless. In the end a production by an auteur director that infuriates and excites the audience, or a professional, well-acted, well-written play that speaks to us are both worthwhile and in short supply. I, for one, would prefer to be infuriated and excited, but I suspect I am in a minority in this opinion.

I didn't intend for this to descend into a jeremiad or a lament for the good old days. What cabaret has brought to theatre and what it can bring back to theatre is a popularity (and populism) that is not at all commercial, but that hits people where they live. Downtown theatre is wonderful, but I sometimes wonder whether its hothouse environment, not to mention the tiny size of its theatres, fosters certain contempt for the audience. Maudlin as it may have been, a piece like *The Vagina Monologues* was popular partly because it spoke of things that were important, dangerous, and titillating to the audience (its rotating cast of celebrities was, of course, the curse of contemporary cabaret performance.) While there hasn't been a recent success on the scale of, say, *Marat/Sade,* the late Rusty Magee and Andrei Belgrader, in *Ubu Rock,* for example, attempted a sort of large-scale, presentational assault on their audience that was amusing, irritating, and ultimately exhilarating. *Hedwig and the Angry Inch* was another piece of this sort. Perhaps the one-person show, where the performative aspect is unavoidable, and the relationship to the audience is essential, has become the last great refuge of cabaret-theatre. Or perhaps it is the drag show—Lypsinka and Kiki and Herb, to name just two examples in New York City—have proven that you can bring drag into the theatre without sacrificing a bit of the savagery of cabaret. Well, maybe a bit. One sacrifice seems clear: Kiki and Herb, and even Lypsinka, are not internationally known, but it is a side effect of the immediacy of Cabaret theatre that it does not lend itself to the launching of international careers, especially in a post-post-modern era.

Obviously, Hedwig owes a debt to the MC of *Cabaret*—both pieces are transparently set in "cabarets," and both guide their audiences through a political journey with the aid of a central, pansexual performer as guide. In both cases, and in the case of all drag shows, the danger is that the characters become picturesque: this has happened to the *Cabaret* MC, who is about as frightening these days as Curly or Nathan Detroit. Lypsinka and Kiki avoid this through the fact that we believe that the performer "is" this character, not merely an actor but a conduit, living the performance. Charles Ludlum, the founder of the Ridiculous Theatre Company, whose plays include the apotheosis of quick-change art *The Mystery of Irma Vep* and a cross-dressing *Camille*, apparently transcended the issue by embodying the melodrama and pathos of his characters so entirely that the camp of his plays was lost in the high artifice. In any case, today's all-out attack is tomorrows' naughtiness. A recent production of *Debbie Does Dallas*, the archetypal porn film, as a live musical event, translated each sexual encounter into a stage-ready choreographed amusement; the result was kind of sweet and not at all dangerous, but is this the ideal mood of a show about a teenage girls having sex with lots of older men? In La Bordas' day, the can-can was a dangerous sexual frenzy; by the end of the century, it was a tourist attraction.

What connects Mae West's drag plays and, say, Wedekind's cabaret sketches, is the idea of making something that both activates the audience and attacks them, entertains but also makes them conscious that they are seeing a performance, with all the things that can go wrong or differently. This is not a play. Who knows what is going to happen?

As a composer, I have struggled with the question of how to integrate the impromptu quality of cabaret with the various possible forms of musical theatre. It is probably the contradictions of the form that excite me the most—between the possibility of disaster and the need for a well-rehearsed performance, between the emotional sweep and even glorious cheesiness of the Musical and the tightness and punch of the political cabaret song. And I must admit, as someone who argues so adamantly for new music and new performances, that I do find myself working in the dangerous gray areas of pastiche and reconstruction more often than would seem healthy.

In my work with the Civilians, a New York theatre company specialising in performance based on actual experience (whether through interviews, research, or other investigation) that is grounded in popular styles and cabaret, I have been trying to explore the possibilities of "new" cabaret-theatre forms, but find myself drawn back to history. The Civilians are partly inspired by Joint Stock, the British company that spawned Caryl Churchill, in whose work interviews with real people on a chosen topic were performed by an actor without notebooks or recording devices, and then recreated for the company. This allows the performative aspect of the interview process to come into the foreground, making it theatrical rather than journalistic. With the Civilians, we have tried to combine some of these techniques with American musical theatre and cabaret impulses, to create a kind of hybrid show. In *Gone Missing*, a show about lost and found objects, a song cycle of loss surrounds real interviews with people who have lost things and made-up radio talk-show footage. The songs play with the idea of style—here Noel Coward, there Mariachi; here Bacharach/David, there Schumann/Heine; here Radiohead, there earnest folk/rock—and while the experiment seems to have been successful, the pastiche nature of the music is probably my way of avoiding the bigger questions of contemporary form and style. Or maybe pastiche is the way forward to a new style.

In *Paris Commune*, a political performance about the socialist rebellion of 1871, the text comes from various pieces of written evidence, rather than interviews, and the songs are drawn, or more accurately, reconstructed from cabaret and opera performances of the era. Most of the songs have been lost or forgotten, so to see them in a modern context can be revelatory, and the songs are incredible, but I am not sure whether this kind of necromancy, however theatrically potent, can help point a way for contemporary stylistic choices. Perhaps, though, it is through addressing the past that some of the problems I am discussing can be solved. It is interesting to see how new these songs—La Bordas's "La Canaille" or Offenbach's aria "Ah, que j'aime les militaries" ("Ah, how I love soldiers!") or Jean-Baptiste Clement's extraordinarily moving and completely forgotten "Mon Homme" can seem in the context of a downtown theatrical performance. In *Paris*

Commune, which I co-authored with Steven Cosson, we are trying to find a way to address the sweep and dialectic of an historical moment, focusing on the events themselves rather than on the specifics of individual people involved in the events. The performative styles of the era—cabaret song, opera, operetta, boulevard comedy, melodrama, bourgeois tragedy, political anthem, popular song—have helped us find a way of performing the anonymity of the event without losing the character of the participants. It is through the performance that the individuality of the Communards comes alive. And this, more than the stylistic quarrel between ancients and moderns, is one way to address head-on the question of how "legit" theatre can incorporate elements of cabaret performance style and content to become a true hybrid form. I wonder whether our work or any contemporary work can recapture the immediacy and danger of La Bordas' performance, even if it recreates the conditions under which it could seem so exciting. We may be living in an era in which the ideal of La Bordas singing "La Canaille," the fusion of song, singer, audience, location, and history, cannot exist in a live form.

I also admit that I am at a loss for what contemporary music style is appropriate for musical theatre, a question plaguing anyone who works within the form. Popular music in America seems to be an endlessly rich area, but whether most of its forms and styles are suited to the specificities of dramatic action is, at this point, as contentious a topic as the issue of contemporary opera. The musical does seem close to the dilemma of the opera in the twentieth century, when it was forced to trade its popularity for the garb of high art, and lost its audience even as much of its work became more sophisticated. For musical theatre, I am not sure if even such talented and "dramatic" popular songwriters as Rufus Wainwright or Stephen Merritt could solve this problem. The form seems trapped between twee sentiment and a kind of arch knowingness—between flavorless sap (as opposed to glorious cheese) and clever nothings. I wish I could say I knew how to write around or away from these problems, but I would prefer to be able to confront them directly.

So, for now, I think what is really needed is a theatre where audiences can relax (maybe they can drink, or, god forbid, even smoke) and at the same time not know exactly what they are in for (in this respect, the tendency of critics to review everything within an inch of its life is a problem). It should be fun, and upsetting, professional but not smooth, unexpected but not esoteric. This is probably not going to happen in the current non-profit theatres, which are so threatened from so many sides that they are forced back on classics and known quantities; it won't happen in the commercial theatre, either, where things have gotten so expensive that they are almost at a standstill, and where the magic of puppetry, shadow play, and circus become *The Lion King*, parody, sketch and chanson *The Producers*, both highly professional and entertaining shows that don't really matter to anybody. La Bordas and May West, Brecht and Charles Ludlum, Busby Berkeley and Larry Hart, knew that they owed this much to their audience, and so should we. The performance *should* matter, even (especially!) when the next day might bring all too real disaster.

Candor and Edge

Jonathan Kalb

First the mini-screed. The most conspicuous cross-fertilization of theatre and film has always consisted in the fact that numerous artists work in both fields. For most of the 20th century, this was inherently neither good nor bad but simply a fact; each world learned from the other, and everyone understood that the two had different demands and expectations. In recent years, however, the learning has been largely displaced by crass opportunism in the commercial theatre. The casting of Hollywood celebrities in serious roles they obviously lack the chops to perform has become a scourge on Broadway.

This cynical practice is now so common that it threatens the one claim to integrity that the commercial theatre plausibly retained during the rise of nonprofit venues: a commitment to superior production values. Brian Kulick, the Artistic Director of Classic Stage Company, has called the inept-celebrity trend 'ecologically the most dangerous thing that has happened to New York theatre . . . It's like a wildlife preserve that's being destroyed.' Normally soft-pedaled in the conglomerate-owned magazines and advertising-dependent newspapers where most American arts journalism appears, this issue received rare prominent attention in November 2003 when the veteran stage and screen actor Ned Beatty, in a *New York Times* interview, explicitly criticised the acting ability of his movie-darling co-stars Ashley Judd and Jason Patric in the Broadway revival of *Cat on a Hot Tin Roof.*

Knowledgeable theatre people have long sniffed at the ostensible talent-drain across the coasts of America, the snatching up of good playwrights, actors and directors by the film and television world soon after they have cut their teeth in the theatre. No worries, say the long-viewers; talented others are born every hour and have no less need for indispensable apprenticeships on the stage. This necessity is precisely what the celebrity scourge calls into question, however. When star-struck critics and audiences alike blink at mediocre theatre work, grave damage is done to the art of theatre akin to the damage done to journalism when big-paper reporters get away with faking sources and inventing stories.

The unequal clout of the theatre, film and television plays a key part in the artistic uses of these media on stage as well. The multiple video projections around the proscenium in the 1995 Broadway revival of the rock musical *Tommy,* for instance, seemed to me primarily intended to reassure patrons in a land where approximately one percent of the population attends theatre that the event was as cool, new and excitingly hyperkinetic as a rock concert or a basketball game. Competition for audiences, especially younger ones, is a harsh reality of our time, and film and video are regarded internationally as sexy accessories to live performers. Even Germany's lavishly state-supported theatres worry about box office receipts, and indeed the most impressive post-Wall success-story there—the Berlin Volksbühne under Frank Castorf, which continues to attract thousands of spectators in their 20s and 30s—has made expensively produced video a trademark of its productions.

Which brings me to my theoretical point: when we speak of film in theatre we almost always really mean video, because nowadays film is invariably used as projected video in the theatre. The distinction may seem unimportant but it has profound implications. Video is watched differently from film, because audiences are aware that video is flexible, relatively inexpensive, and possibly 'live' whereas film, which requires processing and editing, is necessarily a record of past events. Elaborate videos can of course involve as much trouble, expense and editing prowess as film, but my point has to do with expectations. Film presumes a more passive and contemplative relationship to content than video does, especially when juxtaposed with live action, because audiences are never sure whether a pre-recorded video might suddenly switch to a live feed during performance.

This uncertainty is, I believe, a main source of the edgy immediacy in the multi-media work of The Wooster Group, John Jesurun, The Builder's Association, Robert Lepage and La Fura dels Baus. Most theatregoers have never been in a film but everyone has seen themselves on video, if only on security monitors in banks and convenience stores. Both surveillance and the voluntary reproduction of our ordinary and extraordinary moments are inherent aspects of contemporary life, so the interplay of different real-time perspectives offered by these artists often comes off as a sort of hyper-realism. Strangely enough, given video's unsavory reputation for exploitation and invasion of privacy, its use is frequently appreciated as a form of candor in multi-media theatre.

The inherent power of media aside, however, it's also important to recognise that Marshall McLuhan was only partly right when he famously said that new media don't merely record the new world; they *are* that world. The power of all the groups and artists just mentioned also stems in no small measure from the fact that the theatre is not *itself* a medium. It is a live forum in which various media may be presented and/or represented, and the emotional and critical power in multi-media works depend very much on the way those different levels are played off against one another.

In Fred Kelemen's *Desire* at the Berlin Volksbühne in 2001, for instance, an adaptation of Eugene O'Neill's *Desire Under the Elms,* several screens were arranged above and behind the farmhouse set, on which were projected both real-time video of the live stage action and 'alternative' pre-recorded video versions of the same action. In addition, one part of the video reality overtook the live reality after a certain point, in order to underscore the main theme. Once the actress playing Abbie had established her sexual gambit, stoking the desire of both old Ephraim and his son Eben, she ceased appearing onstage in the flesh. For the rest of the play she became exclusively a screen image, a fungible object of desire serving various men's gazes.

In *Ubu and the Truth Commission* (1997) media layering became the source of penetrating social and political critique. A collaboration between the South African visual artist William Kentridge, the writer Jane Taylor, and the Handspring Puppet Company, this piece combined live action with puppets, music, animation and documentary. The text included chilling fragments of actual testimony from South Africa's Truth and Reconciliation Commission, and the different attitudes taken by the play's fictional agents toward both the factual and fictional revelations (in the Ubu story) in the text created what I took to be a composite landscape of witnessing. Oddly, though, the landscape was peopled entirely by perpetrators rather than victims. The interplay of media was used to drain the action utterly of remorse, regret and sentimentality, so that the array of sub-human (read: animated, sculpted and filmed) agents could be submitted for our consideration as the human actors stood by helpless, subordinate, disempowered. All questions of expiation and reconciliation remained conspicuously open.

These are merely indicative examples, of course, chosen from the enormous, and growing, field of multi-media stage work. Whether this is precisely the right trope for the future or not, we are certain to see a profusion of new couplings that defy our powers of description.

Note: This essay was originally written in response to an article by Michael Billington entitled "Stage and Screen," which was published in The Guardian.

It's All About the Audience

Diane Paulus

What interests me about the title of this collection is the very juxtaposition of the word 'popular' with the word 'radical.' In the theatre, we tend not to think about these two words in co-existence. Usually 'popular' connotes crowd-pleasing, entertaining, mass-appealing, perhaps even pandering. It is usually linked to the word 'commercial,' which means 'money maker.'

'Radical' translates into non-mainstream, which usually means non-commercial. 'Radical' is linked to experimental or avant-garde theatre, which, in the last twenty-five years, has been dominated by theatre which is non-linear, non-narrative. It is usually visually arresting theatre, having more affinity with the cutting-edge art world than anything you would ever see on Broadway. More esoteric than accessible, radical theatre often takes on an elitist gloss. It is more often than not heavily subsidised theatre, in which grants and foundation support, not ticket sales, are the financial backbone.

Unfortunately, what we consider radical theatre can feel very un-radical. Something is radical when it proposes an extreme or fundamental change in our way of thinking; when it challenges our institutions, and our habits of mind. Does most avant-garde theatre do this? If we are talking about challenging the institution of theatre, our very habits of theatre –our rituals, and rules of etiquette – then, I would say the answer is no. Why? Because the ritual of theatre is not challenged. It is shocking how narrow our definition of theatrical etiquette is. Essentially, the audience is expected to quietly receive the event, only making noise at solicited moments. The audience is governed by an unspoken code of behavior: pay attention, don't talk to the person sitting next to you, and don't even think about whipping out something to eat (unless food is served as part of the event). Silence is a premium, so unwrap your candies now before the show starts and be sure to turn your cell phones off. And god forbid you ever talk back to the performers – you will probably be escorted out of the premises for misconduct. These rules govern the entire spectrum of theatre, whether you are seeing a Broadway musical, the latest Robert Wilson piece at the New Wave Festival at BAM, a Pulitzer Prize winning Off-Broadway play, or an experimental dance theatre piece in a downtown loft. From what is considered the most "radical" to the most mainstream, these are the rules.

What happens as a result of these rules? The theatrical event runs the very high risk of dying due to the lack of an honest relationship with the audience. We are numbed by conventions of polite applause, of quietly disappearing within ourselves when the theatrical event fails to engage us – creating laundry lists in our head, contemplating what to eat when the show is over, and thinking about anything except what is happening in our very presence. Rather than protest and express our disappointment, we opt to shut down, and fall sleep. The energy in the room becomes one big lie.

I often marvel at actors who blame the audience for a bad performance. 'What a bad audience – they were just dead out there.' Or, 'what a rude audience – they weren't even listening!' I usually take the opposite point of view – what did us on stage fail to do to engage the audience? Why weren't we able to make the theatrical event ignite? As much as the performer can assume responsibility for this failure, sometimes the spectator bears responsibility as well – especially when we start examining the larger factors surrounding the theatrical event which mitigate against the freshest and most honest exchange between performer and spectator. If the audience is stuck in an old habit of mind, even the most radical of theatrical inventions – a play which breaks new form, a musical using a whole new concept - runs the risk of not striking fire.

I would argue we must look for a broader definition of radical theatre. We must go beyond radical form and content to a radicalisation of the relationship between performer and spectator. Theatre will stand a chance of being truly radical if it:

1) wakes up the audience.
2) creates freedom for the audience.
3) breaks all the rules of audience etiquette.
4) positions the audience as a collaborator.

The focus must be on the relationship with the audience. The heart of the theatre is what happens between the performer and spectator; the pulsating, vibrating flow of energy which can only happen live in the presence of both parties. When we make theatre, we must think about the audience. They are our partner. Ultimately, they will complete the theatrical event.

Unfortunately, to think about the audience in the creative process is often considered anathema: you will risk desecrating the purity of your artistic impulse if you start thinking about the audience. For an actor, the dominant training trends of the twentieth century have taught us to forget the audience, to act as if they are not even there. When making theatre with pop forms, you cannot help but think about the audience, because pop forms derive their very 'popness' from the cultural meaning they have for the audience. Because of the audience's familiarity with the pop form's rituals and rules of etiquette, the audience becomes an active partner, or collaborator, in redefining the rules for the theatrical event. All of a sudden, we are no longer limited by existing, and often stifling, theatrical conventions. And it is the audience that takes the lead.

As a director and creator, I have turned to popular forms as a building block for making radical theatre precisely because of the potency that is contained within popular forms for waking up the relationship with the audience. The following discussion examines in detail two pieces of radical theatre which were created with pop forms. The first is *The Donkey Show,* which utilises 1970's disco music. The second piece is *The Karaoke Show,* which taps into the pop cultural phenomenon of karaoke. In both instances, pop forms – disco and karaoke – led the way to the creation of two very striking examples of radical theatre. Both shows were by originally produced

Project 400 Theatre Group, the company founded in 1993 by myself and Randy Weiner.

The Donkey Show

The Donkey Show retells Shakespeare's *A Midsummer Night's Dream* through the world of 1970's disco. The enchanted woods of the Shakespeare play becomes the disco, where, just as in *A Midsummer Night's Dream,* the lovers escape from their real lives to experience a night of dream, abandon, and fantasy. At the most iconic 1970's disco, Studio 54, there was a sense of freedom, of being anyone you wanted to be. It was a Mecca for gays, for the outrageous – people arrived at the club, their entire bodies painted silver or gold. There was what people called 'democracy on the dance floor,' where the average Joe from Queens could rub shoulders with Elizabeth Taylor. There was also unbelievable spectacle – like Bianca Jagger riding in the club on a white horse. And, of course, there were the Studio 54 boys (the 'fairies' of the enchanted woods) who were the shirtless bartenders/bus boys/dancers who populated the club like eye candy. It was also a dangerous world. There was the hustle of getting into the club. The image of hordes of people standing on West 54th Street, waiting to be picked to pass the red ropes, is an indelible part of Studio 54's lore. If you were lucky enough to get in, there were VIP rooms and parties for the inside crowd. Drugs abounded in the stairwells; pills were being popped everywhere. There was even a character known as 'Rollerina' who would skate around the dance floor with a magic wand, giving out drugs from a giant bowl.

One could imagine setting a production of Shakespeare's play in a disco. In fact, I am sure it has been done many times. *The Donkey Show* tells the story of the play without using a single word of Shakespearean text. What became our text was disco music. Originally Randy Weiner, the conceiver and writer of *The Donkey Show,* considered writing new disco songs, essentially creating an original score, following the standard approach for a new musical. For inspiration, he started listening to all the great hits from the period. He discovered that the songs the show needed already existed in the disco canon – perfectly crafted, articulating the entire major story points of Shakespeare's plot. One of the first songs to make it into *The Donkey Show* soundtrack was Thelma Houston's "Don't Leave Me This Way." It was the perfect expression of Helena's dogged pursuit of Demetrius:

> Don't leave me this way
> I can't survive, can't stay alive

Without your love, oh baby
Don't leave me this way, no
I can't exist, I'll surely miss your tender kiss
Don't leave me this way
Aaah baby, my heart is full of love and desire for you
Now come on down and do what you gotta do
You started this fire down in my soul
Now can't you see it's burning out of control
Come on now satisfy the need in me
Only your good lovin' can set me free
Don't, don't you leave me this way, no
Don't you understand I'm at your command...[7]

The world of 1970's disco is defined by its music. Instead of creating watered down 'theatre' versions of disco songs, a decision was made to use the original music from the period. We listened to hundreds of disco songs to select the best songs to tell the story of each moment of the play.

When we did the show in its earliest incarnation, the performers just sang along to the original songs, which were played off records that our deejay was spinning live. It

---

[7] "Don't Leave Me This Way" written by Kenny Gamble, Cary Gilbert, Leon Huff, 1976.

was as if the characters were at a real club: the deejay is playing music, and a song comes on that perfectly encapsulates the emotion the character is feeling. The character is compelled by passion and the moment to sing along out loud. There was much discussion about the validity of this approach. Many of our colleagues from the professional theatre world assumed when we were serious about producing the show in a more legitimate way, we would take out those vocals, allowing the performer's voice to take the lead. What kind of musical is this if the performer is just singing along to Thelma Houston?

In the end, we resisted any suggestion to remove the vocals. Who can sing those disco songs better than the original vocalist, especially if the intent is to recreate the authentic world of a 1970's disco? Would you rather hear Earth, Wind and Fire sing "Hearts of Fire" or a musical theatre performer's version of that song? Luckily in our case, we did not have the best voices of Broadway to confuse our decision. Our company members, who originated the lead roles in *The Donkey Show,* were more actors than singers. The very act of those performers having to meet the likes of Donna Summer wailing out "Enough is Enough" brought their performances to a higher level. It is like playing Shakespeare. The actor is always striving to meet the greatness of the text, of the characters. It is this distance between the ordinary actor, and the greatness of King Lear that makes playing Shakespeare so challenging, so athletic. You are stretched to a size bigger than yourself. Just so with Donna Summer.

The worst offense you can commit when dealing with pop forms in the theatre is to destroy the pop form by watering it down or rendering it unrecognizable, which we would have done, if we had tried to create new disco songs, or employed karaoke versions of existing disco hits. It was a much more radical choice to use the original music as our musical score. It is funny how something as basic as this choice made the piece so hard to define – especially for the critics. *Timeout New York* gave the show a rave review, but asked 'is this theatre?' *New York Magazine* called the piece a 'disco ballet.' *The New York Times* headlined a feature article about the show 'Not Your Mother's Musical,' and wrongly assumed the performers were lip-syncing. At least lip-syncing has a history as a performative style. But something as common a cultural phenomenon as 'singing along' to music – something that we all do in life – in clubs, in the shower, in the car – just didn't have a recognizable place in what we know as the musical theatre.

Using the original music also layers and densifies the theatrical event. At any moment in the show, the audience experiences the music in multiple ways:

1) Remembering a personal moment associated with the song. Hearing the original track reaches outside the confines of the theatrical event, and taps into the memory bank of the audience members' larger lives. Audience members recount to us memories of where they were when they heard the song for the first time, or an emotional crisis that was memorialised by the song. Pop music has that power; we adopt pop music into the fabric of our lives, which give songs a ritual meaning in our lives.

2) Enjoying the music in the present. These are great songs. To hear them blasting over the loudspeakers – to feel the bass pumping in your chest – creates an undeniable Artaudian, sensory experience.

3) Hearing the music in a new way because of the context of the story. Many audience members remark to us 'I never really listened to those lyrics before.' The framing of these songs in the emotional situations of the show's characters wakes up the songs. I remember sitting in a Chinese restaurant during a casting meeting, and hearing Stephanie Mills "I never knew love like this before" being piped in over the radio, and remarking how sick I was of

hearing that song, and that we just couldn't have it in the show. Luckily, I was overruled. It has become my favorite song in the show. The lovers sing along to this song when they wake up to their correct lovers, after all their mistaken love fighting. The lyric "Once I was lost, and now I'm found" has become one of the emotional lynch pins of the show. In the context of *The Donkey Show*, this Stephanie Mills' lyric takes on a surprising biblical depth.

Staging the Show

The Donkey Show had its first incarnation at The Piano Store on Ludlow Street on the Lower East Side. This space was a former speakeasy hidden at the end of a long hall behind an actual storefront piano store. It was a very small room with the delightful feature of a wooden balcony which wrapped around the space. On our most crowded nights, we could fit 80 people in the space. Typically, folding chairs were used for audience seating. Our intention, however, was to create the actual environment of a club, so we immediately removed all the chairs. The audience stood for the whole show, as they would on a disco dance floor. The show subsequently played at the legendary Pyramid Club on Avenue A before moving to the El Flamingo, the nightclub in Chelsea where the show had its official Off-Broadway opening in the summer of 1999. The show has since toured to Edinburgh, London, Madrid, and Evian, France.[8] At every venue around the world, the show has been staged environmentally for every unique club setting. Nightclubs are natural performative environments. In addition to having a stage, most clubs have perches with excellent sightlines, where dancers, performers, or club goers exhibit themselves. There is also the deejay booth, which often assumes a godlike position in the club. The main innovation of *The Donkey Show* set design was the addition of a set of moving disco go-go boxes. These mini-stages are rolled through the audience to various positions around the club, usually with performers on top of them, creating a medieval pageant wagon type of spectacle.

What is most important about the staging of *The Donkey Show* is that the audience is free. They move around during the show. They dance. They drink, and before Mayor Bloomberg, they could smoke. They cheer, jeer, and yell out to the performers. They sing

---

[8] *The Donkey Show*, The Piano Store, NYC, August-December, 1998; Pyramid Club, NYC, January-June, 1999. El Flamingo Theatre and Nightclub, NYC, August 1999-present; Edinburgh International Fringe Festival, Scotland, August 2000; Hanover Grand, London, September 2000-June 2001; Casino d'Evian, Evian, France, July 5-7, 2001; Club Pacha, Madrid, Spain, October 2003-December 2003.

along to the songs. Sometimes a song comes on, and a couple will start making out. We have even had reports of people having sex during the show. If the dance floor is too crowded, you can remove yourself from the action and take a post in the balcony, or if you are lucky, perhaps even get a seat in the VIP mezzanine area. The famous classical pianist, Vladimir Horowitz, used to love to go to Studio 54, and watch people from the balcony. I have always resisted the label interactive theatre for what we do, because it conjures up those awful scenarios of audience members being forced to participate. At *The Donkey Show,* true to club culture, you decide on your level of involvement. If being a voyeur is what you desire, then you take your position on the sidelines. If you would rather be in the thick of it, rubbing bodies with your fellow audience members, then, as in a rock concert, you take your position in the mosh pit.

I have often cited club El Flamingo during a *The Donkey Show* performance as the modern day Globe Theatre, with the groundlings on the dance floor, and the Elizabethan royalty ensconced in the VIP balcony. Tales of the groundlings talking, eating, throwing tomatoes, and transacting business with prostitutes during the performance of a Shakespeare play could not be more removed from what we experience at performances of Shakespeare today. Even at the replica of the Globe Theatre in London, where you can actually be a groundling and watch the show standing in the pit, this does not occur.

Full of anticipation of finally experiencing what it was like to be a spectator at London Shakespeare's Globe Theatre, I bought my groundling ticket to Mark Rylance's production of *Hamlet* in June 2000 only to find myself side by side hundreds of tourists awkwardly shifting their weight from foot to foot during the three hour performance, often looking down at the floor, many finally giving in to their tired legs and squatting besides their knapsacks. When a helicopter passed overheard during one of Hamlet's soliloquies, neither the performer nor the audience acknowledged this interference. Instead, the actor playing Hamlet marched on, the bulk of the speech completely obscured by the roar of the engine circling above. My heart started to race as I contemplated calling out for a replay, exercising my fantasy of authentic groundling behavior. But then I, along with my fellow audience members, remained completely obedient, beaten into submissiveness by our collective theatre etiquette superego. In the end, I left the show, my legs aching from standing at a performance which could have just as well been staged in the comfortable confines of an indoor auditorium with cushy seats.

One caveat: as with the replica Globe Theatre in London, just because you do a show in a nightclub does not make it radical. Too often shows are mounted in nightclubs, but chairs are brought in, programs are handed out before the event begins, and before you know it, as far as the theatrical experience is concerned, you could be sitting inside a conventional proscenium theatre, except perhaps you are allowed to drink a cocktail at your seat. In these cases, the nightclub is being used primarily as an expansion of the set, as in Sam Mendes' revival of *Cabaret* on Broadway which opened at Studio 54 in 1998. What is potentially radical about doing a show in a nightclub is to let a club experience inform the creation of your theatrical event. For instance, when you go out to a club, there is a sense of danger, of spontaneity; a feeling that anything can happen, and that your very presence is significant to and will impact the night's proceedings. There is also profound freedom for the clubgoer – physically, vocally, and experientially. Let these attributes inform decisions as basic as the form your theatrical event will take, and you are on the road to the creation of something radical.

Performing Style

Creating an environment in which an audience feels free to shout out at the performers demands a particular approach to performing on the part of the actor. Being in the moment with the audience is nothing new as a concept – in fact, it is what we all strive for in the live theatre. But the reality of this is a very different challenge. More often than not, performers stick to their pre-rehearsed track, no matter what happens. No one can deny the electricity that shoots through theatre when something goes off track, like when a prop falls off the stage by accident, and the actor has to get it back from the audience. If handled correctly, this can become the high point of the performance. If the actor denies the reality of this event, the truth of the performance is punctured. We know the performer is not really in the present with us, because we have experienced something that the performer denies.

Most theatrical performance is carefully structured, so the performer must rigorously navigate how to take in the audience without throwing off the pre-rehearsed rhythms and timing of the show. In *The Donkey Show,* the performance begins with a pre-show (approximately half an hour) which is completely improvised. Every performer has a clear understanding of what his or her character wants, which in turn, guides their actions. For example, Helen (Helena) wants Dimitri (Demetrius) to pay attention to her. So, she follows him around the club, and tries to dance with him. Dimitri wants to get rid of Helen, so he tries to get away from Helen, dancing with all the women in the audience. The improvisations are endless. Once the show begins, the performers follow set choreography and staging, but how they get from one point to another will always change. Because the performers move through the audience, and the size, shape and nature of the audience changes every night, literally how they get from one entrance to the next is different every night. There is no offstage, no wing into which the performer can disappear and drop character. This constant presence of character allows for all sorts of improvised moments immediately before and after any scene. What holds the performance together is that every performer is striving, in every moment of improvisation, to tell the overall story? So, rather than taking away from the show, every little side moment helps to increase the audience's attachment and investment in the building momentum of the story.

There is one more performance element in *The Donkey Show* that must be mentioned. In the cast, there are four women who play 8 roles. For instance, the actor who plays the owner of the Club, Mr. Oberon, also plays Mia (Hermia), the young lover who has run away to the club to be with her lover, Sander (Lysander), who is played by the same actor who plays Titania, Mr. Oberon's disco-diva girlfriend. There are elaborate quick changes which make this possible. In the curtain call, this doubling of roles is revealed to the audience, which always provokes a shock in the audience, evidenced by gaping jaws, and wild gesticulations of "oh my god, I had no idea!" To play both male and female characters, the performers don a variety of mustaches and wigs as part of their transformation. This is not *Tony 'n Tina's Wedding* which aspires to a filmic reality of environmental theatre, where as an audience, you are made to feel as if you have wandered into an actual Italian wedding. In *The Donkey Show,* the audience is aware they have entered a theatrical space of play. The cross-dressing of women playing men makes the show distinctly theatrical. There is a sense of burlesque with the characters in *The Donkey Show* which clearly invites the audience into a world of ritual enactment. I have watched countless women in the audience flirt and dance with Dimitri, acting out dramas with his character that I am convinced they would not engage in if this character was played by an actual man.

The Karaoke Show

Karaoke is a global pop culture phenomenon. It is a fascinating testament to people's deep and personal relationship to pop music, as well as a demonstration of the essence of performance. In every culture, karaoke takes on different meanings. In Japan, where karaoke was first born, the preferred forum is private rooms, where the performer sings for and with a select group of friends. In America, it is much more common to karaoke in front of a crowd of anonymous people, where the singer can indulge in his or her own personal rock star exhibitionist fantasy. In London, karaoke often takes place in crowded pubs, where the singer is drowned out by a room of inebriated patrons who eagerly sing along. Whatever its preferred form, karaoke fever has caught on around the world.

Randy Weiner and I were interested in creating a theatre piece that used karaoke to tell a story. The story we picked was Shakespeare's *Comedy of Errors*. This early comedy is a farce of mistaken identity centered on a set of twins, long lost brothers separated at birth who find themselves in the same town as grown men. Shakespeare's use of twins points to the underlying metaphysical theme of two halves becoming whole again. In our study of karaoke, this theme found special resonance. When you do karaoke, you find "your other half." The classic karaoke scenario is watching someone transform on stage through the performance of a song. Nothing is more electrifying that watching a sixty year old woman who looks like your typical docile grandmother break out in a hair raising rendition of Janis Joplin's "Me and Bobby McGhee." The beauty of karaoke is that anyone can sing any song. You do not have to look like Michael Jackson to sing "Beat It." As long as you connect to the soul of the song, you can be an Asian woman and tear the house down with this song. An African American man can sing Madonna's "Like a Virgin." Karaoke performance is about transformation. It defies any stereotypical categorisations of gender, sexuality or race.

At *The Karaoke Show,* the audience enters the world of the "Happy Twins Karaoke Lounge" which is designed to replicate an authentic karaoke bar vs. any semblance of a traditional theatre.[9] Strewn on the bars and cabaret tables are karaoke song bibles (books which list all the karaoke songs) and song request slips which audience members fill out if they want to sing. The characters in the

---

[9] *The Karaoke Show*, The China Club, NYC, November 2003-March, 2004; El Flamingo Theatre and Nightclub, March 2004-present.

show mingle with the audience – some as regulars at the bar, some as first timers, and some as employees, depending on their story line. For instance, the hometown twin Anthony (Antipholus of Ephesus) is a regular at the bar, where he is known to cut loose with songs like Nelly's *Hot in Herre*. His twin arrives at the bar for the first time, the soul searching Anthony (Antipholus of Syracuse), who, in contrast to his brother, opts to sing stirring ballads like U2's *With or Without You*. The wife of the hometown Anthony is overcome with passion for this emotional side of her husband she thinks she is seeing for the first time. The shenanigans of mistaken identity unravel from there. The action is told as every character takes to the stage to karaoke. Character is revealed through choice of song. The performance of the song also reveals story, as emotional crises cause breakdowns in the middle of songs. All of the dialogue is crafted to make sense in the public forum of the karaoke bar. We hear lines from the characters when, as singers, they make dedications before their songs, or when, as audience, they call out to the singers on the stage. Our research of authentic karaoke behavior gave us many examples of the natural drama and comedy that occur in a karaoke bar. For instance, witnessing a Wall Street businessman strip off his clothes during his rendition of Elvis' "Now or Never" gave us an idea for how to stage a particular moment in the show. Hearing a woman call out from the audience, 'That's my husband! You're not a cellophane man to me!' during her husband's rendition of "Mr. Cellophane Man", gave us ideas about how to craft the dialogue for the show.

It was deeply important to us that in creating this show we revere the power of karaoke. The worst offense we could commit was to create a theatre event and, in doing so, kill the power of karaoke. Just as in *The Donkey Show*, we made every effort to respect the integrity of the pop form we were using to make our theatre. We looked to the rituals of karaoke to create the theatrical event. From our study of karaoke, we were overwhelmed by the power of the audience becoming one body and singing along with the singer. The collective knowledge of these pop songs makes them like modern day hymnals. In church, if you don't know the words by heart, you can read the lyrics in your hymnal book. In the karaoke bar, you follow the lyrics on the video screen over the stage. We saw the ritual of karaoke as a modern day religion, with a minister hosting the service, calling singers up to the stage to testify. We used this observation to underscore our interpretation of *Comedy of Errors* as a story about the return to the church. In Shakespeare's story, the play ends when the twin brothers seek sanctuary in the local abbey, where they reunite with their mother, who has become a nun. In *The Karaoke Show,* the mother character is the Dragon Lady, the owner of the Happy Twins Karaoke Lounge. After the domestic break up of her family (caused by a storm in Shakespeare's play), she braves the world on her own, creating the Happy Twins Karaoke Lounge as a sanctuary for all those searching for happiness, including herself. She has surrounded herself with all things twin-like in memory of her long lost sons. At the end of the show, she takes off her costume, revealing herself as the mother of the Anthonys who have miraculously found their way to her karaoke sanctuary. A song like Guns N' Roses' "Sweet Child O' Mine" takes on a whole new meaning when Dragon Lady rocks out to it in this context. Her sons recognise her instantly as the mother they never knew: "She's got a smile that it seems to me, reminds me of childhood memories, where everything was as fresh as the bright blue sky."[10]

When the events of the Shakespearean comedy of re-marriage and family reunion have taken place, the show seamlessly segues into its second phase, which we call the 'post show.' It is now the audience's turn to take the

---

[10] "Sweet Child O' Mine" lyrics by Guns N' Roses.

stage. The life at the bar continues as it did during the show, the only difference being that actual audience members are called to the stage to sing. The audience is now ready for their release, having been transformed by the theatrical event they have just participated in. The catharsis of the post-show could never happen at the beginning of the evening. There is an energy that builds throughout the show, like a soda bottle being shook up, that finally explodes when the audience takes the stage. As high as the show goes, the post-show goes higher. First of all, it is completely improvised, and therefore, the possibility for the unknown to occur is present in every moment. There is truly the sense that anything can happen. And anything <u>can</u> happen. An audience member can come up on stage and flop. There is no cult of politeness that will hide this reality. Karaoke is a brutally honest form. It is the ultimate performance test. When a singer connects with a song, it is undeniable. The audience will recognise a great performance immediately – and reward it with unbelievable electric fervor. The room becomes alive, in the moment, for only that moment. It is the ultimate live theatrical event – you have to be there to experience it, to witness it, to participate in it, to shape it.

For the performers, the post-show is a radical extension of the show, where the life of their characters continues in an improvised form. In this way, there is no end to the show. The performers mix and mingle with the audience, as the storylines of their characters continue off stage and into life. There is the opportunity for the audience to literally make contact with the characters. As for the post-show singing, the performers provide spontaneous back up singing and dancing to an audience member's performance, or in some cases, audience members request a specific character to sing with them. The world of the Happy Twins Karaoke Lounge continues beyond any finite world of a play. The pop form of karaoke led us to the discovery of this breakdown of our traditional expectations, to the creation of a radical theatre.

Finally, I end with some guidelines for using pop forms in the theatre. Too often we go to the theatre, thrilled at the promise of experiencing a beloved pop form only to be disappointed. Also, bear in mind, just because you utilise a pop form does not mean that you will create radical theatre. Pop forms have been raped and pillaged for use in some of our most mainstream theatre.

Rules for Using Pop Forms in the Creation of Radical Theatre:

1) Treat your pop culture with ultimate respect. Don't get caught making fun of it. It is a cultural phenomenon – so it is larger than your humble theatrical use of it. It was here before you, and will be here after you. Revere its power.
2) Whatever you do, try not to kill it. What gives theatre a bad rap is when it brags about using pop forms, and then waters down those forms into what we recognise as theatre, but what bears little resemblance to the original pop form. One can think of the countless attempts at hip hop musicals. When was a hip hop theatre piece ever as good as your experience of real hip hop? Perhaps to the small circle of theatregoers, a hip hop theatre piece is exciting, because this audience tends to be completely underexposed to this genre. But the greater audience in America, certainly every kid between the ages of 12 and 16 – the potential theatre audience of tomorrow – knows hip hop for the cultural phenomenon that it is, and will be forever let down by a theatre that doesn't live up to the inventions, wordplay and musical sophistication of most hip hop songs.
3) Take your lead from the pop form. Let it inform and guide your decisions

about the entire theatrical event, including crucial choices about venue, physical relationship of audience, and time and performance schedule for presentation, structure of presentation. Thinking about these elements will actually influence how you create the theatre piece itself.

4) Resist falling back on existing theatrical conventions because they seem overwhelming what should be done, or what we are used to. Do you have to hand out programs before the show, because that is what is usually done? Does a show have to start at 8pm? Does a show have to play Tuesday through Sundays? Does an audience need to sit down?
5) Develop the show in front of an audience. Do not waste your time following the standard developmental process of doing readings and workshops in rehearsal rooms for a staff of theatre professionals. Pop forms need their audience! You will not have a true sense of the potency of your use of your pop form unless you test it in front of audience. The audience will teach you invaluable things. Listen to the audience. Poll the audience. Talk to audience members. Let the audience be

part of the development. A side bonus: your show will develop an audience in an organic way, in tandem with the growing identity of your show. Think of the way a rock band develops. They gig, testing songs in front of sample audiences. They discover what their hits through direct feedback with an audience are. Their identity as a band develops, and they develop a following.

6) Think about who your audience is. The energy of popular theatre, by definition, comes from the audience. And remember, thinking about the audience can lead to the creation of the most radical theatre.

The Karaoke Show (2004). "Mustang Sally (The Courtesan in Shakespeare's "The Comedy of Errors"). Photo credit: Project 400 Theater Group.

Talk Karaoke

Richard Maxwell and Brian Mendes

[Richard Maxwell studied acting at Illinois State University and began his professional career in Chicago, where he was co-founder of the Cook County Theatre Department. Maxwell 'arrived' on the New York theatre scene in 1998 with a production of his play House, which was awarded an Obie Award. Since then, he has presented his work to critical acclaim at distinguished arts venues across the US and internationally. As playwright director and songwriter, Maxwell has developed a signature style of presentation that is defined by an uninflected, declamatory style of acting, a minimalist approach to scenic and lighting design, and an economical use of space. His plays reject the display of emotion exemplified by the naturalistic 'Method' school of American acting, and favour a precise yet strangely nonchalant method where even the most charged dialogue is performed with minimal emotion. Maxwell breaks his texts up with atonal songs that are also presented 'badly' by his actors. His interest as a theatre practitioner is enlivened by what would seem to be 'bad form' to traditionalists, but Maxwell's purpose is to open the playing space to the real, and concrete in behaviour and upend and indeed re-define 'professionalism' in performance. In works like Joe (2002), and Good Samaritans (2004), Maxwell has explored the awkward lives of ordinary American individuals to great effect. His subject is often disappointment and its inevitable pattern on human beings. His plays, which cannot be separated from how they are staged and designed, are the equivalent of post Generation X and Y graphic novels. They chart with stringency, humour and compassion the decline of individuals forgotten by media-hyped US culture, and they serve as piquant reminders of what it means to live a heroic existence against all odds. Maxwell documents American life in an anti-theatrical, anti-'Jerry Springer-mentality' mode. While his work may at times appear off-putting and certainly its lack of seeming affect makes it difficult for audiences to judge whether they should be empathetic to his figures or simply observe them as if under a magnifying glass, Maxwell's intentions are both formalist and humanist. He wants the audience to have a critical distance from his characters but also to engage with them, and be exalted by the performers' presence. Richard has continued in New York and is now the Artistic Director of New York City Players. Actor Brian Mendes has collaborated with Maxwell for over ten years. This

This talk originally took place in a café in Brooklyn, New York. At Maxwell's request, the casual yet somewhat 'performed' nature of his conversation with Mendes has been retained for publication. Special thanks to Jennifer Flores Sternad for practical help with transcription and research, and to the Radcliffe Institute for Advanced Study at Harvard University for space and time. – Caridad Svich]

RM: How do popular forms in performance affect performance in society, such as in the karaoke bar? Is the karaoke bar a truly more alive form of social interaction or engagement than theatre or movies?
BM: Karaoke is a good example because why do people like karaoke? There's no front. You're not trying to be anything different than who you are, but at the same time you're living the fantasy of being a singer, a rock star or whatever. You have your moment in front of everybody, to be the centre of attention, but at the same time there's no pressure to be good, and there's no pressure to be interesting.
RM: Well, there is a little bit of pressure.
BM: Yes, but is it really about you're being 'good at karaoke?' In fact, the bigger the fool you make out of yourself, the more fun it is. Whereas, as an actor, being foolish, being seen as foolish and 'bad,' is not something you want at all. You don't get on stage and think, "Wow

if I make a big fool out of myself, this is going to be really fun." There is a pressure to give a 'good' performance. There are standards and sometimes as an actor, these very standards inhibit your work. I don't like to think when I am in a play about whether I'm good or not. I like to think about what we're doing, what the work demands. For example, if we're going to sing karaoke, I'm just going to get up and try to sing that song, and have a lot of fun doing it. I don't want to be bogged down by issues about what the best way to sing karaoke is or what's going to make me as a performer look good. So, you remove traditional performer pressure, and you're left with: Let me just get through what I have to do, let me say what I have to say, let me sing what I have to sing. Doing the thing becomes the focus, not the outcome.

RM: Do you think it's possible to bring the same attitude and mentality that you have in karaoke to performing in a play? It's hard for me to think of another form where you would have the same set of conditions as you do in karaoke where you have an audience...

BM: Other forms of popular performance are what? Besides karaoke? Conversation? That's not really performance.

RM: I was thinking about chat-rooms: there's a group of people having a conversation, and they're being observed in cyberspace by other people.

BM: That idea of performance is vague. In karaoke you're performing. Is giving a speech performance? Is teaching a class performance? Is anytime you have anybody's attention performance? That gets you into more subtle realms, these areas of performance that you're not conscious of like karaoke, or like--

RM: --Singing on the radio for a contest.

BM: Like when you get interviewed for a radio station, and you know it's being recorded, so there's a sense that the rules are different, whereas--

RM: The medium is clearer too. Not like the internet. If you're just in a room having a conversation or teaching a class it's not really clear. Because the content takes so much—

BM: And the presentation is governed by the subconscious, not by, you know, "I'm doing this because people are watching me," but by "I'm doing this because the content is making me either excited or bored or whatever." Whereas in performance, in stage performance, there are so many contrivances. Which is why it's so hard to do or to pull off—there are just *so many* contrivances. Wooster Group's shows are often just riddled with contrivances: "We can't do this." "We're not going to do this tonight, we just don't have time."

RM: Or, "That actor couldn't make it tonight..."

BM: But at the same time, I feel that they know it's a contrivance and accept it as such, and yet are committed to it at the same time, which adds this layer of perspective that makes it acceptable to me. But I hardly ever see that in theatre. You do, but you're just so, so aware of what contrivances are. I think it's the only way to make something... bearable. The moment someone pretends something doesn't exist, it's not acceptable anymore as performance. It's too affronting, for me, as an audience member, to then take anything else seriously, including the content.

RM: I'm stuck on this idea of bringing the same energy that you have in karaoke to the stage, to that environment. You know, one of the things that I get stuck on is the aspect of commerce that's involved in karaoke. You're conscious as an actor, I'm conscious as a director, that people are paying money to come see our work. But that's not present when you're doing karaoke.

BM: You don't have to give anybody anything. If you really want to serve the audience, you really need to forget about them. For a long time. You know, you can't be dictated by what's going to be worth seeing, 'because that's going to cut out anything that might be worth watching.

RM: Well-- I'd like to separate those. Because you can be very conscious about what it is you want to do and be honest with those impulses that you have inside yourself, and still be conscious of a sense of 'professionalism.' And I put that in quotes. Because you can be honest and yet you can expect that people are going to come and watch it and spread the word about it, so you want it to be as good as it can be. Professionalism is attached to commerce. And I think that might inhibit that karaoke type of impulse from really manifesting itself in staging—in a stage play.

BM: It had been so long since I acted, I had to remind myself not to care about being good. And to go onstage just knowing what I was going to do. I was going to say these words. And people were going to be watching me. I tried to remind myself that any predetermination of how I was going to do these things was the wrong way to go about things. So I guess you could say that in some ways, that's karaoke. You pick the song you're going to sing and you get up there and you're looking at a screen to get the words and then everything else is either a mistake or a trip-up, but there's no preparation. Whereas, as an actor, I know the lines I am going to say. I'm

not looking at a screen, but people are watching me and I have to look at them.
RM: You also have the knowledge that you're going to do it again and again and again--
BM: --And again and again and again. And each time I have to deal with people reacting, which essentially means people making decisions, judging, or whatever goes into reacting to somebody doing something. I imagine a whole series of conscious and subconscious things. It's almost like being a baseball player; I have to stay on my feet to see if it is going to be a ground-ball or a line drive or a pop-up. And that's hard. It's taken me a while to let go as an actor of the tendency to want to be good, to want to *make* something of this, to want to *make* it interesting, to want to *make* it worth their money and worth their time. Those are destructive thoughts. Maybe as a director, as a presenter or plays, as a producer, you are more occupied with such things, but I think the best actors are those who relish what they're doing, who are happy to be there, and want to be there, and want to do it as many times as they can.

We have these preconceived ideas about what art is, and what a good performer is, which is why karaoke is so beautiful, because it negates preconception in a way. You see individuals for who they are in a performance environment. What people do up there, what they perform, is themselves. They're not necessarily trying to play someone else, because they can't be anybody else, because it's not part of the rules, whereas actors have to play someone other than themselves because that's part of the rules of acting and theatre making.

RM: What you want to embody when you're performing, though, is something you could apply to a karaoke scenario.

BM: Well, I'm not very experienced in karaoke. But what I love about it is that people are so focused on the screen, either because they're afraid of looking at people in audience, or so focused on trying to sing the song, that they can't think of anything else. They can't think about trying to be cool, or trying to be good…whereas onstage, generally actors have gotten over their fear of being onstage, so they're occupied with "Am I being good?" And they think it's not enough to be-- I guess I want to say 'themselves,' but what's themselves on stage?

The two experiences I had this year as an actor, the only thing I thought about in terms of normal actor conventions was "How can I do less than what I'm doing?" I feel like I get caught feeling I should do more, so it was a constant reminder to just try to do less. And I don't mean that just as 'less is more,' but I mean that as a meditative state. Get on stage.

Look here. Say this. Move here. That is worthy enough. It needn't be embellished. If you can get comfortable with that, with just simple structures, then a world of possibilities opens up, which I think is more interesting. Whether I ever get there as an actor or not, I don't know, but as for what I would tell another actor, I would say , Just do that, and be ready to see if it's a line drive or a ground ball or whatever and react. Erase any idea you may have about being good or bad.

RM: Is it as simple as there are interesting people and there are uninteresting people and it's simply a matter of taste, whether it's the taste of the performer or taste of the director determining what's interesting.

BM: The idea of star quality has never sat well with me. Though I have said to people, "Well, you're just interesting to watch. So, you win. From the beginning. This is going to work." But it doesn't always work. There are some people who are so interesting to watch that they become uninteresting. They embellish; they're not secure enough. And the only actors that come to mind that are not like that go on stage with such a fear that it's their responsibility to make whatever it is—to make something of it that they ruin the potential that is there through the effort of making.

RM: Is trying to do less-- is *not* making something out of a scene making something

out of a scene? Can you flip it around? Can you flip the negative?
BM: Yes.
RM: I feel that a lot of performance now, a lot of performance that I like, anyway, is about—is good because they *didn't* do XYZ. I've always heard that the acting school golden rule is : "You can't play a negative. You can't do a negative on stage. It has to be positive," but does that need to be re-evaluated now? You said, you don't want to see someone trying to make something out of a scene because they feel like nothing is there, but isn't that in a sense what you're doing? By making the choices that you're making, you're still making choices.
BM: As far as the negative being bad, I disagree with that. Just like I disagree with the idea that drama is the result of conflict. Drama is not <u>just</u> the result of conflict. Conflict can be part of it. I can be fascinated by a play that has no conflict at all. I think that content is always secondary, in my mind, to actors on stage. Or anything on stage. The content is an imposition. They say you start with a space, and you put something in that space. For argument's sake, let's say you put a person in that space, that's where you start. Everything else is an imposition: content, a word, anything else from that point on is a layer, and so, drama is about something in a space. The

closest to that is reality, in the sense of, "We all know what is happening here. We know what's real in this room. We know what's real in this space."

RM: It undermines Brecht; like that idea that Brecht was trying to…that blood would be indicated by red crepe paper, for instance. He was trying to keep people at an emotional distance so they would be able to think, so they would be able to maintain all the faculties of their mind while watching something.

BM: But I remember thinking about that, just that idea of putting people in a position so they can think: it's such a contrivance, because any manipulation like that, to me, just makes me reactionary as an audience member. If I feel like I understand the manipulation it makes me reactionary. If I don't understand the manipulation it makes me reactionary.

RM: What do you mean reactionary?

BM: I mean, if I feel like I'm in a position where, "Oh I need to think about this," I don't want to think about this. I end up shutting off. Whereas if you put me in a position where I feel manipulated, where I have the opportunity to react however I want, emotionally, intellectually, not react at all, whatever—if I feel like it's an environment where there is no pretense or intention, I feel comfortable, and I feel like I want to stay, which is the only kind of theatre that I want to see. Even when you go

to Broadway, or to off-Broadway, and see really good actors, it's a whole other experience to me now. It's like a museum. I love to see them. It's not like I can't appreciate it. But it becomes like an art form that's -
RM: Real static. Why is it that sports events--that's a popular form of expression -- why are they so interesting?

BM: I think that's pretty obvious: because we don't know the outcome. Well, we could say the same thing about watching animals. It's fascinating. You can't pretend to be anything more than you are when you're in the middle of a conflict in a basketball game. Competition. There is an inherent entertainment value in certain forms. Somebody sings, for instance. Either they sing badly or wonderfully or are completely mediocre, but it's always entertaining because there's inherent value in the act of singing. So, what it comes down to is: is there an essence about the self that exists within the play, or there is the intention that you have to *do* something—?
RM: But I think we have to talk about irony then. Irony is parody, which is only interesting to you and is only so interesting. A lot of people think that parody is fine in and of itself. That it's sufficient in terms of performance, its performance value. But I don't think it is. It's

not going to be interesting, for long anyway, if it stays in the realm of parody.
BM: If it's parody then the intention has then been accomplished. Goal accomplished, in other words, and we can move on. And so the question is then how do you make something—if you're singing a song and it's a ridiculous song and you sing it horribly, how is it beyond parody? And the answer has to lie in your commitment to it, and if you are judging it. Don't comment on the text. Don't comment on what's happening. That's the battle as an actor. It's how can you deal with *any* imposition: text, song, dances, any imposition, and not comment on it. Especially when it's something that you wouldn't normally do or are not comfortable doing.
RM: But I want to keep it to irony. Because parody is something else. Parody is something that represents—it's more specific. Irony is broader. Because irony can exist without parody.
Parody is something that is intentional. Irony can exist above intentionality. That is the true battle: getting past irony. There can be an element of sincerity, if that's the opposite of irony, there can be elements of sincerity within an ironic approach. But for me, it's always more interesting when the sincerity outweighs the irony. Irony is what you bring to it, rather than what the performer brings to it. And that

kind of leads me back to the discussion we had earlier today about the notion of Hotspur, the character in *Henry IV,* whose name implies something very clear, very definite and very emotional. Hotspur is an angry guy. How do you play Hotspur without being angry? And maybe a better question is how do you play Hotspur not angry and not ironic? That's why I want to talk about irony as opposed to parody, because that's a tough nut.
BM: If your only intention is to be sincere, meaning, "I need to say these words" then I need to say Hotspur's words. As an actor, saying these words would be the goal; that's my sincerity; that's the realm of my sincerity. I don't mean just sincerely playing anger, or whatever. I'm just going to say these words. If that is your focus, then anything ironic is the situation. It's not pointed to, it's not commented on, it's not played up, it's not ignored. If you stick to the task, then the irony will be limited. There's no way to avoid it, on certain lines. But the general portrayal of the character, I'm thinking will be remembered more as sincere rather than ironic. I feel like the problem with irony is we tend to point to it. Either our insecurity as an actor, or as a director it's just so obvious that inadvertently we point to it. Sometimes we want to show how smart we are, so we want to acknowledge the irony, even subtly.

If you're a song and dance man, if you're speaking, singing, dancing, how do you pull that off? To either make something new, or to comment upon it? Maybe we need to remove this from theatrical boundaries because performance stuff opens so many--

RM: Well, we can look at vaudeville, musical halls, melodrama, operetta, the blues, sitcoms, karaoke, reality T.V....

BM: Why do I hate reality T.V.? I don't know why I hate reality T.V.

RM: I know why I hate it. Why do you hate it?

BM: Because there's this pretense that this is how things are. And that is a pretense, and worse, it's wrong. You know, beyond the fact that there are editors and producers and people selected to get the most dramatic situations, it's so contrived--

RM: The most *natural* situations

BM: Yeah. To me, it ends up being the opposite. It's so contrived and *un*real that it makes this pretense.

RM: At least with scripted shows - what make them tolerable is that you understand the pretense; you know that that you're watching is scripted, you know that it's a sitcom or whatever. But with reality TV you think, 'This isn't scripted, this is real,' but in fact it's just as scripted. You have the added annoyance-- on top of the inanity of it all-- you have the added

annoyance that it's supposed to be real. That it's 'natural.'
BM: What about video coverage of the war?
RM: What about it?

BM: The intention is saying, 'This is what the war looks like,' and in some ways it's amazing. You look at it and: Oh my God, look at this, it's frightening. But at the same time you know it's being controlled. I guess it doesn't have really any relevance to the subject simply because the stakes *are* life and death. In a way that you know you are in college and you're doing the monologue and the instructor says, 'I'll raise the stakes. I'll raise the stakes to life and death.' Still this crazy idea, because it's *not* life and death. It just means be louder.

RM: Tense up more, be louder.

BM: It ignores the reality. Why is there bias and prejudice in society? Is it a lack of experience with the things you're biased and prejudiced against? Or on the opposite case, certain intense experience with what you're biased and prejudiced against?
RM: Both.
BM: If we gain experience through performance it affects our bias or prejudice toward the things we experience. If I have a problem with relationships, I can't have a

healthy relationship. I gain insight from watching the form of a relationship on stage, or listening to songs about relationships, or T.V. shows about relationships. Am I gaining experience from which to make decisions about my own relationship that might alter my bias or prejudice? On some level we have to be validated. As artists or just as an audience. Intellectually, emotionally. Or our obsessions, our fetishes, anything. The things that make us individuals. I've often thought about what entertainment gives me. I kind of always come around to a very general definition of pleasure. Entertainment is what produces pleasure. And that pleasure gets kind of, gets distorted, especially these days where pain can be pleasure. I guess that always was that way, but it seems to be--

RM: It's more complex though

BM: Pleasure's now associated with happiness only. Well, I shouldn't say that across the board. But the denominator is happiness.

RM: Well that's why I consider what I do, the plays that I make entertainment. And I don't think most people would think that.

BM: What do you mean? You have a large following

RM: But I don't think they would call it entertainment.

BM: What would they call it?

RM: Entertainment, I think, more commonly represents what you think of as pop culture, television, and all the things that aren't challenging.
BM: My guess is that a lot of people who are coming to see the kind of shows that you're in, the kind of shows that you do, that I do, are coming because there's an aspect to it that's challenging. So that keeps it out of the generic definition of entertainment because what is entertaining is not supposed to be challenging. It's supposed to give us pleasure. But for a lot of people it is pleasurable to be challenged.
RM: I remember what got me thinking about that was the whole controversy with, you remember that Sensation exhibit at the Brooklyn Museum, and then Mayor of New York Rudolph Giuliani didn't want to keep it running because it was so controversial? It just got me thinking about the relationship between commerce and art.
RM: It's all entertainment
BM: And obviously definitions of entertainment change over years and simple rules of spotting trends would enable us to see that maybe a definition of entertainment that we might share is being shared by a lot of people and that number is growing; our peers, our contemporaries are now aiming for Broadway.

RM: Who would have thought that Suzan-Lori Parks would have a play on Broadway?
BM: It's *hopeful*. Just like in ten years there's going to be two guys who are talking about how what you're doing is old news. That's the beauty of art and entertainment. As the bubble gets bigger and bigger it pops or it gets smaller and something else comes and replaces it. That's why you're in such a good position. Because you're a leader. Whether you want to be or not, you're in a position where people are looking to you to see what you're going to do next. And what you do next matters. That's got to feel good after many years of feeling like it doesn't really matter. Or it only mattered to a couple of people. I remember specifically thinking in the 1980s about how unhappy I was, as young, as a kid, basically, as a teenager; I just felt like there was nothing, no movements happening, nothing really exciting to grasp to.
RM: Were you in college?
BM: I was just graduating from high school and going to college. I felt like there was nothing that I would call interesting. And obviously many people that were my age at that time felt that way because in the nineties things started to happen artistically that I was aware of that was aligned with my aesthetic. That doesn't mean that they were better necessarily, but they were things I could attach to and things to which I could say "I agree."

As much as we argued in the early days, my memory of it was, "Wow, I agree with this guy. This guy knows what he is doing. This is interesting. This is different. This is exciting." Even if, in form, it seems like the opposite. Now I just feel like more people know about it.

RM: Which is good, for more people to know about it?

BM: More can be done. And the more that can be done the more complex it gets.

From Texas, to Virginia: an essay on form

Will Eno

Dear Virginia,

I'm in Texas and Texas is fine. The roads are wide and everybody smiles if you look long enough. There was almost a tornado, the day before I got here, if there can almost be a tornado. There are trees I don't think I've ever seen outside my window. The kids here play like you, maybe more slowly, but nice. You would like it and make friends. I miss you and Massachusetts and everyone.

I'm going to try to answer the questions you sent about your school project for Art. This isn't really my area, but I'll try. I bet there are some books you could read. Maybe there's a movie you could see.

All right, here we go. This should all be hard, but not confusing. Here's some art criticism from your Uncle Will. When the deliveryman judges the painting by the pound or foot, he's only as wrong as a lot of other people. Big canvasses don't necessarily mean big feelings. You asked about what to use and how to use it and what for. What you sort of asked, really, was: What form is the Form, in this day and age (Which is Tuesday and you are twelve). By the way, this is due next Friday? (How long have you known about it?)

Anyway, do this. Start out with whatever little lone-star feeling you have in your good old Virginia self and then go. Don't worry about the rest yet. I say "lone-star feeling" because I said Texas, and said "Texas" because that's where I am. It's Tuesday and I am thirty-eight and in Dallas and I cut my hand getting my luggage out of the back of the taxi. You're my niece and it's raining of all things. I saw a lot of cattle in the rain on the drive from the airport. If I had been older or younger, or it hadn't been raining and the traffic were lighter, or if I were from here and not somewhere else, I might not have been looking so hard; I might not have seen the cows or the one bull looking up into the rain, which was such a human thing to do. See how the day and age helps you out? It practically produces language itself, which can be art, if you look long enough. What you need is usually right there and you just have to turn your head a little, or even less, to see it. Remember how Lucy showed up right after Jolly died? This is the advantage of infinity, of a random endless Universe: there is always something else right behind everything. Love a dog to death, bury it, look out the window to the end of the driveway, and there see Lucy approach, having followed the "Lost Family" flyers. You have a new dog, Jolly is back. The question is almost always the answer.

But, let's get to your project. Let's make sure you get to school on Friday with something other than a piece of cardboard with some spray-painted macaroni glued to it.

Your teacher wanted something different. Well, you're different, Virginia. Who else has that name, "Virginia," Virginia, except the ones who do? Look in the mirror down by the door. See something different, see a Virginia in Massachusetts. Remember our friend David Hancock, from the Bay State by way of The Land of Ten Thousand Lakes? And how we went to see that play of his called *The Race of the Ark Tattoo*? And how it had a sort of flea market in it? Think about that play a while. Remember? If it fell to me to tell a room full of whomever about the origins of that very original play, I would probably say, "A guy named David Hancock wrote it. Now, if you would, hey, just take a look at the guy." See, he's practically a flea market himself. He's different. Say what you want about David Hancock, but he is, always was, and with any luck shall remain, David Hancock. The guy is practically a garage sale, when you look at him. He wrote a play in the form of himself. Took the form of his one and only body and wrote a play out of it, on paper, with his arm and hand. Beautiful guy, really, and beautiful play. Though the body ages as a body, it never gets old as a starting point, as a theme, a source of content. And sure, it came from somewhere else, too, David's play did. Life experience, words he liked, crap he owned, et cet. But the tone is him. The loneliness is him, that kind of scruffy American grandeur, the wrecked lives, the broken toasters, the huge bloody heart, the half-believing in the half-hope of selling everything and moving. So, start in the mirror, Virginia, the meaning's in your wrist, the collarbone you broke, the words that caught your ear, your eyes and the mark where Raleigh bit you that time. (Is Lucy getting walked? Use the leash because I heard they gave Matt a ticket.)

While we're talking about meaning, let's talk some more about it. To worry too much about the meaning of a piece of Art, which you will probably not be making until next Thursday night, is to put the hacksaw before the applecart (Meaning, just forget it, it's a nonsense relation.). See, Virginia, these people with their meaning, all they're doing is replacing one set of signs with another. Yes, in terms of meaning, call *Hamlet* a play about indecision, revenge, guilt, and family-oriented horror. And, yes, in terms of multiplication tables, call the number *Twelve* Two times Six. All done? Well, we didn't really describe, didn't really reckon at all with the blood or bones of *Hamlet*, or the mystery of the number twelve. The thing itself, the play or number, elicits a feeling, a parade of feelings, secret, uproarious, wrong, and all of these, all together, in a constantly shifting array, may be said to be its-- pardon me-- meaning. You are twelve. Are you Two times Six? Maybe you would say you were, because you were always funny, but I don't think you would. Twelve is mysterious enough, complicated enough, the knees all skinned and teasing boys, the private fashion shows, the new views of yourself, the more mature misunderstandings. Twelve is infinite, but don't tell your math teacher I said so. So when you sit down Thursday night, or, Friday morning, forget about the meaning. It'll come later, necessarily, unavoidably. What we have to worry about is the Form, but, don't worry. Two is two and six is six, Virginia, and you are twelve and you have another birthday coming up. Enough math. You asked in your letter, "What's a popular form? Should I use a popular form? Some of the other kids are using popular forms." Second question first: yes, why not, I think you should. But again, keep in mind that you are a form, of a kind. Keep in mind that the body is a form, the self is, an ancient one, and, a pretty popular one, too, when you think about it. And you want this thing, your project, to be "of yourself," or, "of itself," and nothing else. And so, almost necessarily, the true You, if you can find the right way to start, will beget "A New Virginia," and she in turn will yield a form which could be said to be-- because it is true, because it is derived from what is human and true, that is, a human-- a popular form. Is this gobbledygook, Virginia? This is gobbledygook, Virginia, but, I am trying to help and I don't think I'm wrong. Now, second, the first part: what is a popular form to begin with? The question raises questions. Popular with whom? Where? How popular is popular? What is an unpopular form? Anyway, let's abandon those, or answer them with an oversimplification. Pop music is a popular form, for example. The eulogy is a popular form, has been for some time. If you wrote a eulogy for pop music, then you might have something else on your hands. "Friends, Enemies: It is my dazed and melancholy duty to inform you that today, on this fading date in history, this Tuesday of Tuesdays, about an hour before dusk, God, in his infinite wisdom and mystery has decreed, in gentle but irrevocable terms, that that sound we all loved, that happy bubble gummy sound we had come to identify with our snappier halves, with our less-tragic sides, is, henceforth and forever, done, and over, and done. To be replaced from this Tuesday forward by a tolling bell and the sound of a lonely coyote, and a flag snapping in the breeze. Let us bow our heads, for the tambourine, the saccharine lyric, and cross our fingers for ourselves, who remain, in the new and quieter future, with a little bit less than we had before." Do that, take a common form, some common content, and there you go, into the new night, into history, maybe, and difference. Do that and you might have moved into the area of radical expression. It could be that all forms are, at the outset, potentially, equivalent and value-free. They exist, they are out there. Radical expression can arise when a certain form is used to contain and express a certain feeling, within a larger form. Nothing new about the novel, pretty popular form, and, nothing new about a grocery list, ditto, pretty popular. Eggs, toilet paper, paper clips. But, again, another example, if you wrote a novel that was a grocery list: now that would be novel, radical. Or, without making this too complicated, it could be that the radical act is in choosing the particular form in the first place, using it for your own different and particular, light and dark purposes, and, by slowing it up a little, presenting it a little bit sidewise, allowing us to see the feeling that was always in there anyway. There are flea markets and garage sales every weekend. But only one I know of, in a play. *The Race of the Ark Tattoo* starts out expressing what may have been expressed before, but it does so differently, does it so differently in fact, that it ends up expressing something new, that could probably not be expressed any other means or ways. Enough about Hancock. Back to you and form.

We might now ask, what a radical feeling is, and we might feel further far-flung, farther from home, further worried about meeting Miss Charney's Friday deadline. These are difficult matters. Maybe you can get until Monday for this thing. It's simple, too, though. But it's complicated. And finally it's probably dangerous, though possibly necessary, to try to organise feelings into a hierarchy. But it could be that feelings do pretty well at organise themselves, ordering themselves. So skip this whole paragraph.

Remember when you went to London to see that play I wrote called *The Flu Season*. Remember how you cried when you saw your cousin Raquel's hand shaking. It made you cry. You were sad for your cousin and the character she was playing. And you said afterward, "I never knew how sad it was to drink a glass of water." That was a choice piece of criticism, Virginia. We all agreed, but none of us knew it, until we knew. We could have all talked late into the English night until we were gray in the face about popular forms, radical feelings, bookish and unbodily things, and, at the end, when the man said "Time," we would have clarified nothing, predicted nothing. I want you to forget the things they are trying to tell you. It's the body, hurt, sideways, in wonder, marked and scarred with language, in repose, happiness, the body. The animal in the sunshine, the animal in night and rain. It has to be hard for you to understand this at your largely uninjured age. But understand it now, and you will have a jump on the crises and dry spells to come. I am speaking to you as if you will give your life to Art, because I hope you do and think you should. If so, keep always in mind that for the artist to attend too much to talk of this world and its events and the "movements" of the art "community," is like to an astronomer spending his mornings reading of the shabby and over-photographed exploits of teen idols. Remember Raquel's shaking hand. Remember how there was hardly any room for anything else in the Universe. Remember never to forget there is nothing to remember except feeling, how it has inside it all your answers, all your questions, all forms present, past, and future, everything you need to proceed, to the next feeling, the next day, to the new you and real beginning. Start with the body, with sensation and feeling, love everything, eulogise everything, and don't look back, except to look back. As for Friday, anything could work. Without wanting to cause problems, I tell you this: just never do what they tell you to do, exactly. Try, with a good heart, to come close to what they ask for, trusting that because you are you, you just won't get that close, you will still stay far-enough away to stay you, and maybe they will be happy for the difference. Send an essay to your mother, a love letter to your editor; send your fingerprints to a museum. Think feelingly; tell the truth, shrewdly, Virginia; be intelligent, unschooled; elegant, dirty. In this life you barely have enough time to be yourself, so worry not and waste it not in trying to be whatever it is that you think they may want you to be.

I get home on the eighth and I bought you a hat today.

Love,
Will

Notes on Contributors

WILL ENO lives in Brooklyn, New York. His plays have been produced by the Gate Theatre, Soho Theatre and BBC Radio, in London; Sutil Companhia de Teatro, in Brazil; and The Rude Mechanicals Theater Company, in New York. He is a Helen Merrill Fellow, a Guggenheim Fellow, an Edward F. Albee Foundation Fellow, and, was awarded the first-ever Marian Seldes/Garson Kanin Fellowship by the Theater Hall of Fame. His play *Thom Pain (based on nothing)* was a finalist for the 2005 Pulitzer Prize.

MICHAEL FRIEDMAN co-authored *Paris Commune* with Steven Cosson (La Jolla Playhouse). He wrote music and lyrics for *Bloody Bloody Andrew Jackson*, The Civilians' *Gone Missing, Canard, Canard, Goose?* and *Nobody's Lunch*, and Darko Tresnjak's *The Blue Demon* (Huntington Theatre). He has worked as Music Director or Arranger for *The Seagull* and *Cymbeline* (NYSF/Public Theater), *Fully Committed*, LaMama, ART. He was the dramaturg for the Broadway revival of *A Raisin in the Sun*, directed by Kenny Leon. A graduate of Harvard College, he was a 2003 MacDowell fellow.

W. DAVID HANCOCK is the author of *The Race of the Ark Tattoo* and the Obie-award-winning *The Convention of Cartography*. Other awards include a MacArthur 'genius' fellowship, and a Hodder fellowship from Princeton.

JONATHAN KALB is Professor and Chair of the Theater Department at Hunter College of the City University of New York and a member of the Theater Ph.D. faculty at the CUNY Graduate Center. In 1991, he won the George Jean Nathan Award for Dramatic Criticism for his first book, *Beckett in Performance* (Cambridge University Press) and his articles and reviews in *The Village Voice*. Kalb's new criticism collection, *Play By Play: Theater Essays and Reviews, 1993-2002*, was published by Limelight in May 2003.

TODD LONDON is artistic director of New Dramatists. He won the prestigious George Jean Nathan Award for Dramatic Criticism in 1997 for his essays in *American Theatre* and a Milestone Award in 2001 for his first novel, *The World's Room*, published by Steerforth Press. His essay in this issue began as a lecture at the University of Nebraska, Lincoln. It was published in a different form, as "Your Place or Ours?" in *American Theatre*.

RICHARD MAXWELL studied acting at Illinois State University and began his professional career in Chicago. There, he became a co-founder of the Cook County Theater Department. Richard has continued in New York and is now the Artistic Director of New York City Players. His plays are published by TCG. Among his awards are an Obie Award for his play *House* in 1999.

BRIAN MENDES is a founding member and former artistic director of the Cook County Theater Department in Chicago from 1992 to 1997. He has worked with Richard Maxwell both in Chicago and New York for over ten years.

DIJANA MILOSEVIC is one of the founders and director of DAH Theatre in Belgrade, Serbia. She is also director of DAH Theatre's International School for Actors and Directors and permanent collaborator of Magdalena Project-an International Network of Women in Contemporary Theatre.

DIANE PAULUS is Artistic Director of American Repertory Theatre in Massachusetts. She has directed for Chicago Opera Theater, and at the Brooklyn Academy of Music, both with British conductor Jane Glover. She is the director of the *Donkey Show,* which has toured internationally, and played in an open run Off-Broadway, and directed revivals of the musical *Hair!* and the opera *Porgy and Bess* on Broadway.

SARAH RUHL is alumna playwright at New Dramatists in New York City. Her plays include *Eurydice, The Clean House, In the Next Room, Passion Play* and *Late: A Cowboy Song.* Among her awards: the Susan Smith Blackburn Prize, the Helen Merrill Award, Whiting award, and finalist for the 2005 Pulitzer Prize. She is a MacArthur Fellow.

ALEKS SIERZ, author of *In Yer Face: British Drama Today* and *The Theatre of Martin Crimp.*

NINA STEIGER joined the staff of London's Soho Theatre as Director of the Writers' Centre.

CARIDAD SVICH is alumna playwright of New Dramatists and a former Radcliffe Institute Fellow at Harvard University. She is editor of *Trans-Global Readings: Crossing Theatrical Boundaries* and co-editor of *Theatre in Crisis?* (both for Manchester University Press), and *Out of Silence: Theatre & Censorship* (Eyecorner Press). She has also edited books on theatre and performance for TCG, Smith & Kraus, and BackStage Books.

Other selected NoPassport Press titles include:

Envisioning the Americas: Latina/o Theatre & Performance
Migdalia Cruz, John Jesurun, Oliver Mayer, Alejandro Morales, Anne Garcia-Romero. Preface by José Rivera. ISBN: 978-0-578-08274-5

Migdalia Cruz: El Grito del Bronx and other plays. Preface by Alberto Sandoval-Sánchez. ISBN: 978-0-578-04992-2

David Greenspan: Four Plays and a Monologue. Preface by Taylor Mac. Introduction by Helen Shaw. ISBN: 978-0-578-08448-0.

John Jesurun: Deep Sleep, White Water, Black Maria – A Media Trilogy. Preface by Fiona Templeton. ISBN: 978-0-578-02602-2.

Carson Kreitzer: SELF DEFENSE and Other Plays. Preface by Mark Wing-Davey. Introduction by Mead K. Hunter. ISBN: 978-0-578-08058-1

Matthew Maguire: Three Plays. Preface by Naomi Wallace. ISBN: 978-0-578-00856-1.

Octavio Solis: The River Plays. Preface by Douglas Langworthy. ISBN: 978-0-578-04881-9.

Saviana Stanescu: The New York Plays. Preface by John Eisner. ISBN: 978-0-578-04942-7.